He was staying the night. Though her invitation hadn't exactly been gracious.

Dane noted the furrow between the woman's brows and the tight compression of her mouth, which still somehow managed to look sexy and inviting. She wasn't happy with the arrangement.

He wasn't certain he was either.

He did need medical attention, but that wasn't the reason for his trepidation when it came to staying the night. The rest had to do with the woman standing before him. She made him nervous as hell.

Because he'd never responded to any woman quite the way he was responding to Regina Bellini.

Dear Reader,

What is an honorable man to do when he finds himself falling in love with a married woman? That's Dane Conlan's dilemma in *Saying Yes to the Boss*.

He knows he's smitten the moment Regina Bellini opens the door to her house and thinks he's someone else. He *knows* who she is, even though they've never met. After all, destiny requires no introduction. But the road from "Hello" to "I do" is not smooth for this pair. I've made sure of that. For the final installment of my CONLANS OF TRILLIUM ISLAND trilogy I have paired a woman who is ashamed of her passionate nature with a man who is bound by his honor.

Ree has stayed in a loveless marriage because it is safer than exploring the emotions that led to her mother's mistakes and ruin. Dane knows that acting on his desire will come at the cost of his self-respect.

Let me know if you like how it all works out. Contact me at www.jackiebraun.com.

Best wishes,

Jackie Braun

SAYING YES
TO THE BOSS

Jackie Braun

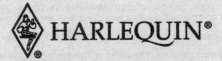

TORONTO • NEW YORK • LONDON
AMSTERDAM • PARIS • SYDNEY • HAMBURG
STOCKHOLM • ATHENS • TOKYO • MILAN • MADRID
PRAGUE • WARSAW • BUDAPEST • AUCKLAND

ISBN-13: 978-0-373-03905-0
ISBN-10:   0-373-03905-0

SAYING YES TO THE BOSS

First North American Publication 2006.

Copyright © 2006 by Jackie Braun Fridline.

Jackie Braun earned a degree in journalism from Central Michigan University in 1987 and spent more than sixteen years working full-time at newspapers, including eleven years as an award-winning editorial writer, before quitting her day job to freelance and write fiction. She is a past RITA® Award finalist and a member of the Romance Writers of America. She lives in mid-Michigan with her husband and their young son. She can be reached through her Web site at www.jackiebraun.com.

For my big brothers, Bill, Jim and Tom,
and in memory of Danny.

CHAPTER ONE

REGINA BELLINI WAS expecting company.

When she heard the knock at the door, she set aside her glass of Chianti, slid her feet into the soft leather heels she'd picked up during a trip to Italy and stood. Anticipation hummed through her body as she smoothed down the fabric of a slim-fitting skirt and carefully retucked her white silk blouse.

As she passed the gilt-edged mirror that hung in the foyer, she paused to check her appearance. She fussed for a moment, pushing the tumbled mass of dark curls back from her face. Humidity had made a mockery of the hour she'd spent that morning blow-drying her hair straight. Still, she looked presentable.

And so she picked up the shotgun.

It wasn't loaded, which was a pity she decided as she eyed the man's silhouette through the oval of stained glass on the old Victorian's front door. The double barrel, however, made quite a statement. Raising the gun, she swung open the door and pointed its business end directly at the man's broad chest.

"For the last time, I'm not selling," Regina said, hollering to be heard over the storm that had turned the July night chilly and inhospitable.

"And I'm not buying, lady," the man promised, stumbling back a step.

It was not quite nine o'clock but it was nearly pitch-black outside thanks to dark thunderclouds. Lightning cracked as he spoke, illuminating the scene more clearly than did the meager light that burned overhead on the generous expanse of porch. In that brief flash, the shock on the man's face was unmistakable. It registered right along with the fact that he was handsome as sin and not the pesky developer Regina had been expecting.

"I thought you were somebody else," she sputtered in surprise.

"Yeah, I got that." The stranger's deep voice sounded strained, but it held a hint of amusement. He motioned toward the gun. "Mind pointing that thing someplace else?"

Regina hesitated. He was soaked to the skin, short dark hair plastered to his head. Yet even wet he exuded that same cocky sense of self-assurance she had come up against a little too often lately. She tilted her head to one side and asked, "Are you a developer?"

His dark brows tugged together in an incredulous frown. "Are you going to shoot me if I say yes?"

"You'll have to answer the question to find out," she challenged.

The man divided a considering look between Regina and the lethal weapon she still gripped.

"No, ma'am," he said solemnly and held up a hand as if he were giving an oath.

It was then that she noticed the blood. Bright crimson, it leaked down his arm from a gash across his palm.

"My God! You're hurt." Regina quickly set aside the gun and reached for him, tugging him partway into the foyer for a better look. "What happened to you?"

Despite the fact that the stately home was perched on a narrow point of land that jutted into one of the Great Lakes, his reply was the last thing she expected.

"Shipwrecked."

Then his eyes rolled back and he stumbled forward into her arms in a dead faint, the weight of him taking them both to the floor. More than six feet of man lay on top of her—more than six feet of a wounded and unconscious man. His bulk made it impossible for Regina to scoot far enough inside the house to kick the door closed with the leg that wasn't trapped between his thighs.

The rain was coming down in a furious assault now, the wind slanting it sideways so that it marched with ruthless precision across the covered porch's wood floor and then doused them both with its chilly spray.

The man moaned and, coming to, raised his head slightly from where it had come to rest after their fall: facedown between Regina's breasts. He stared into the gaping V of her blouse for a long moment before transferring his gaze to her face.

Concussed or not, he had the nerve to smile.

"Given my position, I probably should introduce myself," he said, the words slightly slurred.

Was that a dimple denting his cheek? She fought the

urge to be charmed by either it or the bemused humor lighting his otherwise bleary eyes. How could he laugh at a time like this? A year from now, *ten* years from now, she might recall this bizarre situation and find it funny. Right now she had to settle for being mortified.

That was an emotion that didn't sit well with Regina, which is why her tone was clipped when she replied, "No, given the position of my left knee, you probably should get off me. *Now.*"

He slipped obediently to the side, grunting with the effort. Once on the floor, he rolled onto his back and groaned in earnest.

"Are you okay?" she asked, feeling slightly guilty about her less than sympathetic treatment of him. "Do you think you can sit up?"

He ignored her questions, pointing out instead, "Do you realize that you've threatened me with great bodily harm twice and I don't even know your name?"

Oh, yes, she definitely felt guilty.

Generally speaking, she wasn't an insensitive woman, much less a violent one. But the persistent badgering and—lately—veiled threats from a local developer had definitely taken their toll on her manners. Still, this man needed medical attention. At the very least, he deserved to be brought in out of the damp night air.

Oh, what Nonna Benedetta would say if she were still alive. Regina's Italian grandmother had been such a stickler when it came to offering hospitality to houseguests, whether they had come to her door invited or not.

"I'm Regina Bellini. Friends call me Ree," she said as she stood and attempted to adjust her clothing.

Blood was smeared across the sleeve of her now soggy blouse, the top button of which hung by a useless thread. She pulled the lapels together in an attempt at modesty, which seemed absurd given the fact that the man's face had been pressed into her cleavage mere minutes ago.

He must have read her mind. His gaze dipped low before he made eye contact again. Awareness sizzled, as dangerous as the electrical storm blowing in off Lake Michigan. Maybe it was only the man's supine position that made the situation seem so intimate.

"It's nice to meet you, Ree. I'm Dane Conlan."

He struggled to sitting with her help, and she was finally able to close the door, which he then leaned against, looking thoroughly exhausted from the effort.

In the foyer's more generous light she could see that his plain white T-shirt was covered with grime and blood, and the jeans he wore were ripped, exposing one battered knee. He'd apparently lost his shoes and socks, assuming he'd worn them in the first place. His feet were bare and covered in sand and other natural debris from his hike up the dunes that bounded the lake. What she could see of his toes appeared puckered from his time in the water.

"You said you were shipwrecked," she said, crouching beside him.

"In a manner of speaking, yes. My boat hit some rocks, went down about half a mile from shore. I was coming across from the island, but I got blown off course a bit."

"I'll say. The main dock is five miles south of here as the crow flies," she said. Her own paralyzing fear of water had her asking sharply, "What were you thinking, taking a boat out in a storm?"

He shrugged, but looked chagrined.

"The weather wasn't that bad when I started out and Trillium is only a few miles out from the mainland," he said, referring to the large island visible from the docks in Petoskey. On a clear day, it could be seen from the point on which Ree's house stood sentinel. "I figured I could make it to shore before things got too ugly."

When she merely raised an eyebrow, he said defensively, "I would have, too, if the engine hadn't quit on me. I started to drift. I radioed for help, but by that time the boat's hull was already kissing rocks, so I decided to swim for it."

"You're lucky you didn't drown."

He regarded her intently for a moment.

"You saved me."

"What?"

"I saw your lights and kept swimming toward them. I thought I was having a near-death experience." One side of his mouth lifted in a grin, mitigating the soberness of the moment. "Is this heaven?"

Despite the frightening picture his words conjured up, she couldn't help herself. She smiled in return. The man's charm was downright lethal.

"No. And neither is it an emergency room. I think I'd better call an ambulance."

"Don't. I'm fine." He attempted to stand and then sank back to his knees on a groan. "I just need a minute," he muttered.

Ree was a bit more pragmatic in her assessment of

the situation. "You're bleeding and you passed out. You need to see a doctor." Raising an eyebrow for emphasis, she added, "It's obvious you've hit your head. You appear delusional."

"God, you're something else."

He wasn't the first man to tell her so. In fact, the developer she'd been expecting that very evening had used the word "unbelievable" modified by a most foul expletive when she'd spoken to him by telephone earlier in the day. But Dane Conlan's tone seemed to turn the words into a compliment.

"Just let me use your phone," he said. "I've got friends in town. I'm sure one of them can come get me."

She relented with a nod and then helped him to his feet.

"I would offer to drive you, but my car is in the shop," she said.

"That's okay. I don't want to be any more trouble than I've already been."

A man who didn't want to be any trouble. In Ree's personal experience members of the opposite sex only rarely had been anything but.

When he stood, Dane weaved precariously for a moment before finally leaning against her for support. He wasn't overly tall. In her heeled shoes she was only half a head shorter than he was, putting him just over six feet. Nor was he thickly built, edging more toward wiry than stocky. But the hand she placed around his waist as she helped him into the Victorian's parlor was touching taut muscle.

A fire burned cheerfully in the hearth. She guided him toward the wing chair positioned closest to it, and forced herself not to think about what the man's wet, grimy clothing would do to the upholstery. She had more pressing problems than soiled cushions or Dane Conlan, who would be gone from her home soon enough. Then she picked up the telephone and bit back an oath.

"Don't tell me," he said, apparently noting her grim expression.

She set the receiver back in the cradle. "Storm must have taken out the line."

"I don't suppose you have a cell?"

"It's in my car."

"The car that's in the shop?"

"That would be the one."

It galled her to think about her yellow Volkswagen Beetle—a refurbished original rather than one of the newer models—sitting uselessly on a hydraulic lift at Hank's Collision & Repair. Regina had argued with Hank earlier that day over having to pay for a loaner when this was the second time in a month her car had been in because of its faulty starter. Finally she'd stomped out and caught a ride back to Peril Pointe with one of the mechanics. Temper had cost her the rental of a cheap replacement vehicle as well as the use of the cell phone she'd left stowed in the car's glovebox.

"How far is town? Maybe I can walk."

"Seven miles by road." She crossed her arms over her chest as she regarded him. "On a night like this and in your present condition, I don't think it would be wise."

"Neighbors?" he asked.

She shook her head. "Nearest house is three miles south of here. I'm afraid Peril Pointe is rather remote."

Which was precisely why developers were clamoring to buy it. The house was situated on the most western tip of seven acres of premium property fronting Lake Michigan. It was prime real estate. The yearly taxes alone put a strain on Ree's currently limited budget.

He blew out a gusty breath and settled back in the chair. "Well, then, unless you're going to turn me out into the storm, it looks like I'll be spending the night."

She watched his gaze detour briefly to her ruined blouse. Once again awareness lit his eyes as he offered that charming smile that had a single dimple winking low in one cheek. The man could have been on his death bed and she would bet he'd still find the energy to flirt with the nurses.

Ree glanced at the framed photograph of Nonna Benedetta that was perched on the mantel. Her grandmother had been a delightful woman with a firm belief in duty and enough patience to deserve beatification.

With a sigh of resignation, Ree replied, "I guess so."

I guess so. Not exactly a gracious invitation. Dane noted the furrow between the woman's neatly arched brows and the tight compression of her mouth, which still somehow managed to look sexy and inviting. Regina Bellini wasn't happy with the arrangement.

He wasn't certain he was, either.

He did need medical attention. Not necessarily the trip to the E.R. she had suggested, but the gash on his hand could use a few butterfly bandages—okay, maybe a stitch or two—and his head felt as if the entire drum section of the high school's marching band was using it to pound out a cadence.

But those weren't the only reasons for his trepidation when it came to staying the night. The rest had to do with the woman standing before him. She made him nervous as hell and it didn't have anything to do with the fact that she'd leveled a double barrel at his chest.

He'd never responded to any woman quite the way he was responding to Regina Bellini. She was beautiful, lushly so with that cloud of dark hair, generous mouth and a pair of heavily fringed eyes that held enough secrets to keep members of the opposite sex curious.

And he was curious, although some things he already knew. She had a body built to complement a man's: not quite slim, not overly curvaceous, but definitely soft and yielding in the places that mattered most.

More than her array of appealing physical attributes, however, he admired her sheer nerve. This was no shrinking violet, no damsel in distress. She'd answered the door toting a gun, for God's sake. He grinned at the recollection. Who knew that having his life threatened would prove to be such a turn-on?

And he was turned on. Despite the brutal physical abuse Mother Nature had meted out during the past couple of hours, his libido was humming along in over-drive. Amazing. Absolutely amazing.

"Is it a private joke or are you going to clue me in?" Regina asked, apparently having noted the slight quirking of his lips.

"Just can't get over my luck today," he replied smoothly. "I cheated death. Twice."

Her expression turned contrite as she knotted her fingers together. "About that. I want to apologize for the way I answered the door." She cleared her throat. "I've had a little…trouble lately."

"With developers?" he guessed, recalling her questions about his occupation.

"Yes."

"Apology accepted." When he started to ask about the trouble, though, she shook her head.

"It's nothing I can't handle."

Lightning flashed then, followed by a serendipitous clap of thunder. When the sky was dark once again, so was the house, except for the flickering fire. Dane was beginning to think the woman could handle anything. Other than muttering an oath in what sounded like Italian, Regina Bellini didn't miss a beat. She found a box of matches, lit a couple of candles in the hurricane lamps on the room's antique tables and rolled another fat log onto the fire.

Dane decided the only thing left to do was joke about their lousy luck.

"I must have done something to tick off the gods. Do you believe in fate?" he asked.

The woman apparently wasn't in a joking mood. She regarded him for a moment before answering his question seriously.

"I believe we're responsible for our own situations, our own destiny. No matter what life throws at us, it's ultimately up to us to find a way to deal with it and make the best of it."

"Lemonade from lemons?" he asked and she nodded.

That had long been Dane's philosophy as well. Too

many people he knew expected something for nothing or complained copiously rather than rolling up their shirtsleeves and getting down to business to change what they didn't like.

Dane put his faith in hard work and perseverance. Both yielded results. But, thinking back on the hour he'd spent bobbing around in the waves of Lake Michigan before being spat onto the shore at Peril Pointe, he decided maybe luck played a role, too. How else to explain his presence in the beautiful Regina Bellini's front parlor?

Lemonade from lemons.

"I like lemonade," he murmured. His gaze lingered on her pursed lips. "Sweet is nice, but tart is better."

She shook her head and sighed heavily in exasperation. But when she spoke, her request had his mouth going dry.

"Take off your clothes, Don Juan."

He blinked and on a startled laugh replied, "Well, that certainly would be making the most of a bad situation, but gee, Ree, I hardly know you. I like to take a woman out to dinner first, maybe see a movie, before we spend the better part of the evening—"

He wasn't able to finish the sentence before she tossed a crocheted afghan in his direction. It wound up draped half over his head.

"Your clothes are wet and filthy, Mr. Conlan," she said. "You need to get out of them, and I'm afraid that afghan is about the only thing around here that's going to fit you unless you'd prefer to wear my bathrobe."

"Call me Dane. And, just for the record, I prefer to remove women's garments, not put them on."

She made a little humming noise that might have been the result of annoyance or reluctant amusement.

He scooted to the front of the chair and peeled off the damp shirt, using the cleanest edge to wipe up the blood drying on his arm.

"I'm messing up your upholstery," he said and grimaced. "And your clothes. Hope that blouse wasn't one of your favorites."

Her expression seemed to soften. "Well, it's not as if you planned to faint in my arms."

Planned? No. He considered that a little side bonus given his lousy day. Still, he cleared his throat, feeling the need to clarify, "Men prefer the term 'passed out.'"

He was pretty sure she was smiling when she turned her back to him.

"The rest of your clothes, please."

Dane stripped down to bare skin, handing over the remnants of his favorite jeans with a sigh of regret, and then he wrapped the afghan around his body toga-style. When she was gone, he tried to stand without holding the mantel for support. He wasn't quite successful, but he felt far better than he had an hour ago when he'd washed onto the beach, coughing up water, his arms, legs and lungs burning from the effort it had taken him to get there.

He hadn't been teasing her about following the Victorian's lights. They were all he'd seen, those and a light on some structure closer to the shore, beacons of hope that had kept him putting one arm in front of the other as waves tossed him and currents tugged at him with disorienting force. Now those lights were gone as well thanks to the storm. He shivered at the thought of what would have happened to him had the electricity failed earlier.

"I can get you another blanket if you're cold."

He hadn't heard her return, but he glanced over to find her standing next to him, brows furrowed in concern. She'd changed into a pair of capri pants and a pullover that was probably some pastel shade, although he couldn't discern its color in the firelight. Her feet were bare and the ponytail she'd swept her hair into exposed the graceful line of her neck. She looked younger, softer. And yet he still felt it, that insane blast of attraction that had him wondering if he'd struck his head harder than he'd thought.

"Dane?"

He realized he was staring and coughed. "No, I'm fine. The past few hours are catching up with me is all."

"I'm sure. You had quite the ordeal."

In her hands she held a first-aid kit and a bottle of painkillers.

He nodded toward the bottle. "Got anything stronger than ibuprofen?"

The smile she offered was sympathetic. "Sorry, no, but I had just opened a really good bottle of Chianti before you knocked at my door. I'm willing to share."

"You don't have anything with a little more…kick?"

As a general rule, he wasn't one to wallow in the false comfort of hard liquor, but he could do with a good bracing belt of whiskey right about now.

"You probably shouldn't even have wine," she told him, sounding almost prim. "But I'm feeling indulgent. Sit."

She didn't wait for him to comply, but gently nudged him back into the chair and then knelt on the floor in front of him.

"Let me see your hand."

Dane did as Regina instructed, deciding he could do with a little TLC and pampering after all he'd been through. Then he sucked in a sharp breath along with an oath when she dabbed the cut on his palm with enough stinging antiseptic to kill half the bacteria in the free world.

"God! Blow on it or something," he begged between gritted teeth.

"That would defeat the purpose of disinfecting it."

His eyes were watering. His hand was on fire. "I'll take my chances. A nasty case of gangrene has to be less painful."

He leaned over to blow on it himself. When he looked up afterward their gazes held. The air seemed to sizzle as he watched the firelight reflected in her dark eyes. She had questions, too. He saw them there. And it came as a huge relief to discover that he wasn't the only one mired in this odd, instantaneous need.

The moment stretched before she finally looked away and muttered, "Men are such babies."

"You're not going to start in with that argument about how if it were up to us to give birth the human race would have ended with Adam, are you?"

No hint of feminine interest remained, but he felt sure he hadn't imagined it. She smiled at him with the same smug superiority he'd often seen on his sisters' faces.

"No. We both know which one is the weaker sex. Why rub it in?"

Then she ran the cotton swab of antiseptic over his broken skin again.

Dane decided to change the subject. To take his mind off the pain, he asked, "So, what have you got against developers that makes you keep a shotgun handy?"

"You mean besides the fact that the one I've had to deal with lately is greedy and unprincipled and only interested in buying Peril Pointe so he can tear down my home and put up condos or another high-priced resort that will make that snooty Saybrook's on Trillium look like a pauper's retirement community?"

She was affixing butterfly bandages across the ravaged skin of his palm during her vehement response and Dane grimaced. No way in hell he was going to admit to her that in the most basic sense of the word he *was* a developer or that he and his two sisters actually owned the resort she'd referred to as "that snooty Saybrook's."

So, when she finished her minidiatribe, he worked up what he hoped was a charming smile.

"I'll take that wine now, please."

CHAPTER TWO

THE grandfather clock chimed out the hour as they sipped their wine. It was only ten, but it seemed much later. Indeed, it felt as if hours had passed since Regina first opened the door to find a drenched and injured Dane Conlan on the other side of it. With the electricity out and no phone service for who knew how long, it was clear she wouldn't be saying goodbye to her handsome houseguest anytime soon.

The thought had her bringing the glass of Chianti to her lips again and drinking deeply.

Two years had passed since Ree had spent an evening alone in the company of a man. The last encounter had ended with a screaming match inside a tent pitched in the Nevada desert. Actually "match" wasn't the word for it as Ree had done all the screaming, peppering her accusations with the Italian curse words she'd heard her grandfather using when Nonna Benedetta was out of earshot. None of the verbiage had gotten a rise out of the recipient. Paul Ritter had barely managed to look up from the dusty dig log he so meticulously kept to respond.

"Let's talk about this later, Regina."

That had been Paul's mantra throughout their previous five years of marriage, during which Ree had followed her archaeologist husband from one godforsaken dig site to another. Each time he'd promised this one would be the last and he would get a teaching post at a university. Ree wanted a home of her own. She wanted to start a family.

Two years later, she was legally separated and had filed for divorce. Paul had yet to sign the papers, not because he wanted to make their marriage work, but because he just hadn't gotten around to it. She knew that because the one time she'd managed to reach him by telephone, he'd admitted as much, right after which he'd launched into an excited monologue on his team's most recent findings. His work, once again, took precedence.

Regina hadn't pressed the issue. Why rush failure? So she remained in limbo. Now she wondered, was that any better?

She glanced over at Dane. She barely knew him and yet in the span of a mere hour she'd already formed the opinion that he didn't believe in postponing trouble or confrontations. No, he seemed the sort who faced whatever came along when it came along—from a sinking boat to a raging electrical storm to an angry woman aiming a firearm at his heart.

One broad shoulder poked from the afghan her grandmother had knitted a half-century earlier. Even the cover's mauve-and-pink squares couldn't detract from his masculinity. In the flickering light she noted the firm musculature on what she could see of his chest, arms and legs. More than good genes, it took discipline to get a body that looked like that. Ree respected discipline as long as it didn't snuff out all spontaneity.

She glanced up then and realized he'd been watching her study him. Clearing her throat, she asked, "Are you hungry or would you rather just go to bed?"

His slow smile seemed to fan the heat that was flooding into her cheeks.

"I'm famished."

It was Dane who spoke and yet Ree found herself moistening her lips. Another kind of appetite whetted as she repeated, "Famished."

He winked then. "Yeah, but first I'd like to clean up a bit more, if that's okay with you?"

She'd brought him a damp washcloth and towel after bandaging his hand, not trusting him to stand long enough at the bathroom sink to wash his face. But she could appreciate his desire to rinse off more of the grime.

"Of course."

He leaned on her once again, putting one arm around her shoulders and holding the flashlight she'd provided in his good hand. With shuffling steps they followed the bouncing beam through the darkened house to the powder room just off the front parlor.

"Fresh hand towels are in the cabinet over the toilet," she told him as he braced against the pedestal sink. Noting his hunched posture, she added, "I'll wait outside the door just in case you need me."

Ten minutes later, she helped him into one of the ladder-back chairs at the table in the home's large kitchen. His face and upper body were freshly scrubbed, and his

hair was as neat as his fingers had been able to make it.
Ree hid a smile as she realized that Dane now smelled
like the lavender rosettes from the guest soap dish. Then
she sobered when he turned his head slightly and the
rough stubble of his beard grazed her cheek. Certainly
nothing else about the man could be considered
remotely feminine.

She lit a few candles, including the one in the cen-
terpiece on the table, and the scents of cinnamon and
ginger mingled pleasantly as she moved about the
familiar room, completely at ease despite the poor
lighting. Ree had grown up in this house. Every squeaky
floorboard and stubborn windowpane was committed to
memory. Of all the massive house's rooms, this was her
favorite and thanks to her grandmother's patience, Ree
was a good enough cook to do it justice.

If houses had hearts, the kitchen was the Victorian's.
Life pulsed from here. That especially had been true
when her grandmother was alive. Even now, as Ree
stood in front of the late nineteenth-century cabinetry
that unfortunately was starting to show its age, she could
almost hear Nonna humming a Dean Martin tune, the
blade of her knife making quick work of a bulb of garlic
for pesto. It would pain her grandmother that the wood
still needed resurfacing and more than a few of the door
hinges begged for replacement. Ree had not been able
to make those repairs or the many others the home
required. Regret came swiftly, but she pushed it away.
She swore she heard Nonna's voice whispering to her
that it was impolite to dwell on her own troubles when
she had a guest to feed.

"The stove is gas, so it still works. I don't have much in the fridge at the moment. I'd planned to go grocery shopping today, but…" She shrugged.

"No car," Dane guessed.

"Exactly. So, grilled cheese and tomato soup okay with you?"

"Sure."

She pulled a loaf of homemade bread from the old-fashioned metal box on the counter. As she sliced it, she asked conversationally, "So, tell me a little about yourself."

"What do you want to know?"

"Let's see…" She mulled her answer as she slathered butter onto the bread and transferred the slices to a cast-iron skillet. It was appalling, but the question she wanted to ask was if someone special was waiting for him, worrying over him, back on Trillium. She had no right to ask such a question. No right to even *want* to ask it.

She settled on the more generic, "Why don't you tell me about your family."

"I've got a couple of sisters, Ali and Audra. They're twins." He grunted out a laugh then. "Of course, they're nothing alike in either looks or personality."

Ree sent him a smile over her shoulder, ridiculously relieved that he hadn't spoken of a wife and kids. "That must be nice. I always thought it would be fun to have a sister or two."

"An only child, huh?"

"Not exactly." She stirred water into the pan of condensed soup she'd opened. "I have two half sisters and a half brother, but…we're not close."

Not close? The sad truth was Ree had never even met

them, and only knew of their existence thanks to an entry in a diary she'd found that had belonged to her mother.

"That's too bad."

She decided to redirect the conversation. "So, tell me about your sisters. Are they older, younger?"

"Younger, but that doesn't keep them from trying to run my life." There was a smile in his voice despite the complaint. "Ali tried to talk me out of coming over to the mainland for supplies. She wanted me to wait until the morning."

"Smart woman," she replied pointedly, giving the soup another stir before flipping the sandwich.

"Yeah, and I can guarantee she's not going to let me forget it. Neither of them will once they find out I'm okay." He cleared his throat. "Wish that could be sooner rather than later. My sisters are probably pacing the floor."

His voice brimmed with remorse. The tone told her that family was important to him. Nothing was more important, Regina knew, and so she couldn't help but admire Dane Conlan's priorities. Not everyone put family first. Her husband clearly wasn't willing to, and her father hadn't. Or, at least, Ray Masterson hadn't put the family Regina was a part of first.

She lowered the heat on the soup. Glancing over her shoulder again, she said, "It's nice to have people who care enough to worry about you."

"What about you? Who's worrying about Regina Bellini?"

No one. The sparse reply echoed painfully through her head.

Since her grandmother's death after a long battle

with congestive heart failure several months earlier, Ree had been completely alone. And lonely. *So lonely.* Tears threatened now and she was grateful that, in the low light, Dane could not see her blink them away.

Even so, she turned back toward the stove, stirring furiously for a moment as she collected her thoughts. "I'm pretty much on my own," she said at last, amazed that her voice sounded so normal.

She no longer had any immediate family—at least none that acknowledged her. Nor could she count on any close girlfriends. Maintaining meaningful relationships with other women had been difficult when she'd lived like a nomad for half a decade and then had returned to her hometown with her marriage in tatters and the only person who could be of any comfort wasting away in a nursing home bed.

Ree had moved Nonna back to Peril Pointe and hired a private nurse. Between the two of them, they had tended to the fragile, elderly woman until Benedetta Bellini drew her final breath. During those dark and painful months, even if she'd had friends, Ree wouldn't have had time for them.

She heard both surprise and sympathy in Dane's voice when he asked, "What about your folks?"

"My mom…died when I was six," she replied vaguely.

Ree half expected Dane to ask her how. She wasn't sure what her answer would be, which was strange. She'd never even told Paul the details of her mother's death beyond saying Angela Bellini had drowned. Suicide was an ugly family secret, one she'd long chosen to keep.

But all Dane said was, "God, I'm really sorry. And your dad?"

She chewed her lower lip for a moment. Another ugly family secret, and yet she found herself sharing this one.

"My mom never married my father, so he wasn't around when I was growing up."

She did keep the more painful details to herself, such as the fact that the real reason Ray Masterson had not wed Angela Bellini after the scared and pregnant eighteen-year-old had showed up at his doorstep was that he was already married and the father of two children with a third on the way.

"That had to be tough."

"It was a long time ago," she said, trying to sound as if her father's disavowal of Ree's very existence didn't still wound her to the core.

"So, who raised you?"

"My mom's folks. Great people." She smiled now as she dished the soup into a blue porcelain bowl and put the sandwich on a matching plate.

"Are they still living?"

"No. They're both gone. My grandfather passed away during my senior year of college. My grandmother died last Thanksgiving."

As she set the meal in front of him, Dane surprised her by reaching for her hand. The pad of his thumb rubbed over her knuckles in a negligent caress that still had her breath hitching. "God, Ree. I'm really sorry."

She stared at their hands, wanting so desperately to turn hers over so she could weave her fingers through his and simply hold on. It felt so good to be consoled, and, God, how she missed being touched. Her grand-parents had demonstrated their love with frequent hugs, kisses and pats to her cheek. Paul had run hot and cold with his displays of affection. When a dig was going well, he'd sometimes surprise her with an embrace. If not, days could pass without so much as a brush of fingers against her arm or a chaste peck on the cheek.

"Thank you," she replied hoarsely. Maybe it was only because Dane was still holding her hand that she admitted, "I really miss them, especially Nonna. She was something else."

"Nonna?"

His hand fell away and Ree took the seat opposite his at the table. "It's Italian for grandmother."

"Tell me about them?"

It came out a question and because he seemed gen-uinely interested, Ree did.

"Nonna and my grandfather came over from Naples just after the Second World War. My grandfather worked in an automobile factory in the Detroit area and my grandmother stayed home raising my mother. When my mother was a girl, they came north for a vacation and stayed at Peril Pointe. The people who owned it rented out rooms and my grandparents returned every summer after that. My grandfather decided to retire early and they used their savings to buy the house and move here."

"Did they run it as a bed-and-breakfast, too?"

She shook her head. "No. I think they planned to. They took in guests here and there, and they loved meeting new people. But then my mom died and they wound up raising me."

"They sound like incredible people."

"They were. And very much in love." She smiled at the memories that always warmed her. "When my grandfather was still alive, he and Nonna would go for a walk along the beach every evening in the summer. They always held hands."

Ree had envied them that. Their grand, sweeping love affair had spanned more than five decades of marriage, while even the most tepid of emotions hadn't been evident just a few short years after her and Paul's wedding day.

"I can't imagine that kind of love," she murmured.

"My sisters seem to have found it," Dane said thoughtfully after chewing a bite of sandwich.

"They're both married?"

He nodded. "And Audra's expecting her first baby in the fall. A girl. The doctor says she'll arrive around Halloween, but if the kid is anything like Audra, she'll be so stubborn she'll hold out till Christmas."

Interesting, but beneath the humor she thought he'd sounded almost wistful. And so she asked boldly, "What about you? Have you found that kind of love?"

Dane had spooned up a mouthful of soup as Ree spoke. Then he nearly choked on it as the name Julie Weston blasted into his brain with all the subtlety of a stick of dynamite detonating. It was the first time he'd thought of his girlfriend since arriving at Ree's. He acknowledged that truth with a stab of guilt, followed swiftly by regret, because he knew that neither the knot on his head nor his near-death experience was the real reason she'd failed to show up on his mental radar.

Everyone kept telling him how perfect Julie was for him. After nearly three years of dating, he'd be the first to admit she was a fantastic woman: smart, funny, pretty in an understated sort of way. She cooked a mean beef stew, could carry on an intelligent conversation and was the ideal euchre partner, never reneging or failing to take a trick with trump. But too often he found himself wishing for a loner hand and thinking that something was missing.

One question haunted Dane: *Was this all there was?*

Ali had Luke. Audra had Seth. Both couples seemed to have hit the mother lode of happiness. They deserved their bliss. Dane didn't begrudge them a moment of it. But as they feathered their new nests and made plans to start families, he felt envious, and maybe even a little empty.

He was thirty-five, settled and successful. During the past few months he'd begun to agree with Julie: Time was ticking away and they weren't getting any younger. Yet marriage to her seemed utterly anticlimactic, an epilogue rather than an exciting new chapter in his life. He had enough respect for the institution that he didn't think it should be that way.

"When are we going to make it official, Dane?" Julie had asked him the question that very afternoon. He'd had no answer for her when he'd left Trillium, so eager to escape that he'd foolishly headed out into a storm on the pretext of getting supplies that the resort hardly needed posthaste.

He glanced across the table at Regina Bellini. God help him, but he did have an answer for Julie now, and it wasn't one she was going to like. But how could he make a lifetime commitment to one woman when in the space of a couple hours a virtual stranger had helped convinced him that would be a huge mistake?

Love at first sight? Nah. No way. But something was going on here. Something disturbing enough that it had caused him to forget completely the woman with whom he had been inching toward matrimony.

"Well?" Ree asked.

He blinked. "S-sorry?"

"I asked if you've managed to find that kind of love."

The candle flickered briefly between them on the tabletop, the dim light making the room intimate as the revelation in his head slipped past his lips.

"No," he said. "Not yet."

They talked for another hour sitting in her homey kitchen. Thunder rumbled in the distance, but the storm was moving off. Dane credited the food, the painkillers and a second glass of wine for the fact that he no longer felt so shaky and weak. He credited Regina for the fact that he was actually enjoying himself on what undoubtedly had been one of the worst nights of his life.

"Well…" Ree stood and began gathering up the dishes. After depositing them in the sink, she said, "You're probably getting tired."

"Not especially. I'm a bit of a night owl," he admitted. "Besides, I read somewhere that people who take a blow to the head shouldn't go to sleep—at least not alone. Something about the possibility of lapsing into a coma."

He couldn't resist flirting with her and he enjoyed immensely watching one side of her mouth quirk up.

"I think that's an old wives' tale," she replied dryly, but she settled back onto the chair opposite his.

She didn't rise again for another two hours. By then, they both were yawning.

"I'll show you to your room," she told him as she blew out the candle and flipped on the flashlight.

Dane pulled the afghan more securely around his midsection and stood. Even though he felt steady on his feet, he didn't object when she drew near to assist him.

For the past couple hours they had talked companionably about everything from the right way to eat French fries—doused in mustard rather than catsup—to whether the Detroit Lions would ever manage a winning season. Neither would bet on it. Beneath the newly established camaraderie, awareness had simmered. Now, as he walked with her through the quiet house, that awareness returned to a rolling boil.

"I think you'll be most comfortable in here. This is the only one of the seven bedrooms located on the main floor."

Ree opened the door and Dane knew right away that it was hers. The light bewitching floral scent had him inhaling deeply. In the dim light he eyed the big four-poster bed with its fluffy down comforter and then cleared his throat.

"This is your room."

"Yes."

"Where will you be sleeping?" It came as quite a surprise to realize he was holding his breath after he asked the question.

"I'll be in the first room to the left at the top of stairs."

When he started to protest, she shook her head. "I'll

be perfectly comfortable there. It's the room I slept in before my grandmother died. Besides, I don't think you're ready to navigate stairs in a strange house in the dark. I'll feel better with you in here."

"Thank you."

"You're welcome."

She was still standing beside him, one arm wrapped loosely around his waist. It took little effort for Dane to turn until they were facing one another. When he bent, he intended only to brush a kiss over her cheek, but she turned her head slightly or maybe he turned his. Either way, his mouth settled over hers and the chaste peck graduated to a kiss full of curiosity.

Still, he might have pulled back and managed to bank the need, but she made a soft moaning sound in the back of her throat that had the same effect as pouring kerosene on a campfire. Heat flared and good intentions were forgotten. He framed her face with his hands. He had to do something with them, because if they were allowed to roam any lower he knew he would be doomed.

And that was before the afghan wrapped around his waist tumbled to the floor right along with the flashlight she'd been holding.

The kiss ended on his strangled laugh and Ree was chuckling as well when Dane rested his forehead against hers.

"I seem to have lost something," he said at last. "And you, too."

Oh, Regina *knew* she'd lost something. Forget the flashlight, she'd lost her mind. This was crazy, foolish and she wasn't the sort of woman who did crazy, foolish things. She'd toed the line her entire life, eager to spare her grandparents the worry and grief her mother's impulsiveness had caused.

Thinking of them, she said, "I'd better go."

"Yes. You should."

But he didn't release her and she found herself almost glad. It felt so good to be held, to be wanted. It took all of her willpower to finally step away—and to keep her gaze level with his before she turned toward the door.

"I'll leave the flashlight with you. Good night, Dane Conlan," she called over her shoulder when she reached the threshold. "Sleep well."

He laughed, sounding bemused, and she thought she heard him mutter, "Yeah, like that's going to happen now."

Alone in the room upstairs, Ree lit a candle, tugged the dustcovers off the furniture and dropped heavily onto the side of her old bed. She'd never been this wound up or felt this…this physically aware. She scrubbed her hands over her face, amazed by and a little ashamed of her body's reaction.

As she made up the bed with fresh linens, it dawned on Ree that she'd forgotten to grab a nightgown from the dresser before leaving Dane in her room. She wasn't fool enough to tempt fate now by going back for it, so she stripped off her clothes and climbed into bed wearing only her underwear.

With a tortured sigh she realized that was one garment more than what the handsome man tucked between the sheets downstairs had on.

CHAPTER THREE

WHEN Ree descended the stairs early the next morning after dressing hastily in the cropped pants and pullover she'd worn the evening before, the scent of frying bacon greeted her. She found Dane in the kitchen standing in front of the stove, his hair wet from an apparent shower and a bath towel hooked low around his waist. A bouquet of bruises bloomed on the middle of his back, but that wasn't the reason she sucked in a breath. The same outrageous tug of desire she'd felt the night before was still there. It hadn't moved off with the last of the rain. And she still had no idea how to deal with it.

She cleared her throat. "Good morning."

Dane turned and offered a smile, revealing that solitary dimple that had haunted her dreams.

"It's better than a good morning. It's a *great* morning. The sun's shining. Birds are singing. I'm alive."

Despite the offhanded way in which he said it, she got the feeling he truly meant it. Glancing out the window at Lake Michigan, she remembered the way the waves had heaved and bucked against the shore the evening before. The great lake was calm right now, but it could be brutal and unforgiving under the temper of a storm. He was indeed a lucky man.

"I take it you're feeling better."

"Much." He nodded toward the frying bacon. "I hope you don't mind, but I rummaged through your fridge and decided to start breakfast."

She swallowed hard. A gorgeous, half-naked man was standing in her kitchen preparing a meal for her. He'd even made coffee.

"I could get used to this," she murmured and then was pretty sure she blushed. She couldn't believe the direction her thoughts were taking. To hide her consternation, she asked, "Finding everything okay?"

He nodded. "You have an amazingly organized kitchen. Everything is right where it should be. Well, except for the coffee."

"You didn't find it in the canister marked *Coffee?*" she asked dryly.

"I found it, but the grounds hold their freshness longer if you keep them in the freezer."

Regina got down a mug from one of the cupboards and poured herself a cupful of the beverage in question. "I'll take that under advisement," she said on a chuckle as she stirred in some nondairy creamer.

She leaned against the counter and watched him flip the sizzling strips of bacon with a fork. He looked completely at ease in the kitchen, obviously no stranger to the workings of a stove. Taking a sip of coffee, she nearly sighed. He made a mean cup of joe on top of his other culinary skills. It was scary how the marks in the man's plus column just kept mounting.

Although she didn't mean to compare him to Paul Ritter, she found herself doing just that. Her husband didn't know a coffee pot from a roasting pan. He had always been too distracted by his work and too disinterested in the mechanics of meal preparation to offer to cook her breakfast. He'd never so much as poured her a bowl of cereal. Ree's gaze strayed to the towel around Dane's hips. Moistening her lips, she admitted that Paul had never looked quite like that while wearing terry cloth, either.

The toaster popped up and she jumped right along with the delivery of two pieces of evenly browned bread. She wasn't a woman to let passion overrule dignity and decorum. Nor was she a woman ruled by impulse. That had been her mother, with disastrous results. Ree wasn't like Angela. She'd made a point of proving that her entire life. As for last night and that kiss, it was but a momentary lapse brought on by stress and the storm.

"Everything okay?" Dane asked.

She smiled to hide her embarrassment. "Barely a sip of coffee and I'm already jumpy." As he buttered the toast, she added, "I see the electricity came back on."

"Yep. About six this morning."

"I wonder if that means phone service has been restored as well."

He shook his head. "Sorry. I already checked for a dial tone. Nothing."

As she watched, he cracked an egg one-handed into a skillet of melted butter. The man was a regular

Wolfgang Puck. Her grandmother would approve. To Nonna, cooking had been on par with praying.

Although he appeared as at ease as she wielding a spatula, good manners compelled her to ask, "Is there anything I can do to help?"

"Nah. I've got everything under control. And cooking breakfast is the least I can do after everything you've done for me."

"I really didn't do that much," she demurred.

But Dane grinned. That solitary dimple flashed briefly in the stubble on his jaw, and her pulse shot off like a damned emergency flare.

"You did. More than you know." Before she could ponder what he meant, he asked, "So, how do you like your eggs?"

"That's an easy one. This morning calls for sunny-side up."

Just as she had the night before, Ree found herself seated across from Dane at her kitchen table. The conversation flowed surprisingly easily given the way his gaze would sometimes linger on her lips. In the bright morning light Ree realized that his eyes were an interesting cross between gray and blue, and they definitely clashed with the green and purple welt protruding from his temple.

"You'll need to see a doctor today."

"I know. When the phone comes back on I'll make an appointment right after I call my sisters to let them know I'm okay."

"You'll probably need stitches."

He glanced at his bandaged hand. "Possibly."

"And maybe even a tetanus shot."

His lips twisted into a grimace. "Yeah, that's a possibly, too."

"Do you think they'll recover your boat?"

"I don't know how much of it will be left to recover." Then he shrugged. "I've got insurance. It wasn't fancy anyway." He glanced around the kitchen. "Not like this house. I didn't get a chance to appreciate it last night with the lights out and my head on fire."

"That's understandable."

"The detail work is incredible. I'm guessing it was built in the late 1800s, probably between 1885 and 1890."

"Eighteen eighty-seven," she confirmed, surprised by his perception.

Motioning with his fork he asked, "Do you know if those are the original cabinets?"

"Yes. The hardware is vintage, too." She frowned at the worn finish of the cabinet doors and tarnished brass knobs before her gaze dipped to the scored floorboards that peaked from beneath a faded throw rug in front of the stove. "I'm afraid most of the house could use a fresh coat of paint and other renovations."

Ree could afford none of that right now. She would be lucky to scrape together enough money to pay the taxes when they came due in the fall. Her grandmother's long illness and then Nonna's request that both she and her deceased husband's bodies be interred in the family plot in their native Italy, had depleted not just her grandmother's bank account but Regina's limited savings as well.

Dane lifted his shoulders in a shrug. "That's cosmetic. The structure appears good."

"For the most part," she agreed. But since the house was all she had left of her family, it pained her to see it in such shabby condition. "It needs new shingles, though, and part of the floor on the side porch is a casualty of dry rot."

"Basic maintenance," he said with another shrug, unaware that Ree had been racking her brain for months trying to figure out how she could afford those necessities. "Get it fixed up and you could turn it into a world-class bed-and-breakfast. The view alone would have customers lining up at the door."

"I've thought about that," she admitted.

She had more than thought about it, actually. But opening her home to paying overnight guests still required an initial investment. It would take money—and a lot of it—to whip the Victorian into the kind of condition it needed to be in to attract high-paying clientele and hire the required staff. In the meantime, the bank wasn't likely to extend that kind of credit to a woman who had no stable source of income or track record for running such a business.

It was breaking her heart to think that despite all her efforts, she might wind up selling the place after all.

Dane's low whistle pulled her back to the conversation. "Did you know that your banister is made of quarter-sawn oak? They don't make homes like this grand old lady any longer."

"No, they don't, which is why I don't want to see it destroyed by some developer who isn't as interested in preserving history and beauty as much as he is in making a quick buck."

"So don't sell."

She wiped her mouth on a napkin as the familiar panic settled in.

"It's not that easy. I own the place outright now. My grandmother left it to me when she died. But the taxes…" With a sigh, she slumped against the back of the chair.

"Steep, I'm sure, especially for this much frontage on Lake Michigan."

"And especially for me at the moment." It galled her to admit, "I'm sort of between jobs."

Actually she hadn't had a steady job in years. During the time she'd tagged around after Paul, she had worked as a freelance writer for a travel magazine. The pay was decent when she sold something, and living out of a tent, or at times a small trailer, had kept expenses pretty minimal. But her journalism degree hadn't seen much of a workout since she'd returned to Peril Pointe. In any case, even with the aid of a nurse, caring for her grandmother had been a full-time job. Ree now had her résumé in with the local newspaper and a northern Michigan magazine. But even if she secured full-time employment, the aging Victorian with its constant upkeep and eye-popping taxes would remain well beyond her budget.

Dane watched the shadows play across Regina's face. She was obviously torn, despite the fact that selling the house would turn a tidy profit for her, assuming there were no sizable liens to be paid off. But Dane could appreciate the sentimental attachment she had to her grandparents' home, especially since she had nothing left of her family now.

"So, who's the developer that's been sniffing around?" he asked.

He knew most of the local ones, a lot of whom were genuinely nice people. Maybe he could serve as an intermediary and help Ree work out a solution with the one who had been giving her such a headache.

"Bradley Townsend," she replied.

Dane didn't realize he'd issued the expletive until Regina glanced at him sharply.

"Do you know him?"

Oh, he knew him and he wouldn't mind going a few rounds in a ring with him. The guy was a snake. A couple of years earlier he had put in a bid on Saybrook's when it came up for sale. When that hadn't worked he'd tried to seduce his way into the resort the Conlans had nursed back from the brink of bankruptcy by romancing Dane's sister, Ali.

"Watch yourself around him," Dane warned. "The man has the scruples of an alley cat."

"What do you think the gun was for?" Regina asked dryly and her tone had him grinning.

"I like your style, lady." He laughed, his gaze lingered on the full lower lip that he'd sucked gently the evening before. Swallowing hard, he said seriously, "I like *you*, Ree."

"Well, I did save your life."

"It's more than that," Dane insisted. Surely it had to be. He set the fork aside and pushed back his plate so he could lean toward her. "Tell me you don't feel it."

"Dane, about last night—"

But Dane wanted to get this out. He'd had several

hours to consider the new direction he wanted his life to take after being quite literally blown off course on his way over to the mainland.

"I'd rather talk about this weekend. I have some… loose ends to tie up," he said, thinking about Julie. He planned to break things off with her that very day, regardless of Ree's answer. But he hoped her answer would be yes. "I want to see you again, give whatever this is a chance to develop." She was already shaking her head when he added, "We can take it slow if you'd like."

Regina wanted to say yes. She did indeed feel the crazy need or attraction or whatever else it might be that seemed to be constantly buzzing in the air around them. Standing in a darkened bedroom or sitting in a sunlit kitchen, she felt it and it terrified her.

Besides, as tempting as she found Dane Conlan, the timing for a new relationship was all wrong. Emotionally, so much of her life was in upheaval. And then there was the not so small matter of her marital status. Paul had yet to sign and return the papers that would dissolve a marriage that had been in name only for the past couple years.

The fault wasn't only his. Ree had dragged her feet as well. At first, she had not pressed the issue because she'd been so busy tending to her grandmother. Then Nonna had gotten wind of the pending divorce and frail as she'd been, her disappointment had been evident.

"You've made a vow to your husband," Nonna had told Ree. "You made that vow before God. Salvatore and I had to make plenty of adjustments during the first years of our marriage. All couples do. Promise me you'll try to make it work."

Ree had promised, although she hadn't tried exactly. But neither had she gone ahead with the divorce in Paul's continued absence, even though her lawyer had advised her that would be her right.

Now, how to explain her current not-quite-divorced state to the man whom she had allowed to kiss her so thoroughly the night before? She got up on the pretext of refilling her coffee cup.

"It's not as simple as taking things slowly," she began.

Dane was on his feet as well, crossing the room until he stood just behind her. He took the mug from her and set it aside. His hands were in her hair then, gathering it up and lifting it away from her neck.

"I think it can be that simple."

His breath heated her skin just before he kissed her nape. Afterward, Ree turned and coherent thought fled when he placed his hands on the countertop on either side of her waist. She was trapped between his solid build and the equally hard surface of the cabinets, a shamelessly eager prisoner. So much for his offer to take things slowly. So much for her decision to rein in her passion. When he lowered his head, she was lost, as swamped as he must have been during his doomed boat ride across from the island.

God, she wanted him. It was the only reality that registered amid the urgency of his kiss. She gave up, gave in, winding her arms around his neck and holding on fiercely as his hands left the safety of the tiled countertops to caress the small of her back. When his fingers gathered up the hem of her shirt and inched it higher, her body temperature rose as well, spiking feverishly.

"This is crazy." She moaned as his good hand worked to free the back clasp on her bra.

"Insane," he agreed, nibbling her neck.

Ree had never felt this desperate, this out of control. Had it been like this for her mother, she wondered dimly before the thought was lost to a fresh surge of desire.

"I've never—"

Dane's mouth plundered hers again. "Me, either."

"I want—"

"I know."

And she reached down to help him pull her shirt over her head, eager for skin to meet skin.

From the corner of her eye she spied the man standing on the other side of the kitchen door, his serpentine smile quite evident despite the pane of warped glass. At her hoarse scream, Dane turned as well and then let out a rabid string of curses.

"I don't believe it," he bit out. "Bradley Townsend has a bad habit of turning up where he's not wanted."

Ree wanted to die. Even if the other man had not had a ringside seat to what had just occurred in her kitchen, her swollen lips and the whisker burns on her neck would have been a dead giveaway. More damning, of course, was Dane's state. The towel he was wearing couldn't hide his arousal.

Ree took a deep breath, hoping to regain as much of her composure and dignity as possible. She smoothed down her shirt and tucked her rioting hair behind her ears.

"Where's my shotgun when I need it," she said, muttering curses in Italian as she crossed the room.

She yanked open the door with an air of authority she didn't quite feel given the fact her bra was not hooked and her knees still felt like rubber.

"I think I've made it clear you're not welcome here, Mr. Townsend."

"Just checking to see how you weathered the storm." His capped smile was about as sincere as a shark's. Then he glanced past Ree and his expression turned even colder and more calculating.

"Conlan, I'm surprised to see you here."

Dane crossed his arms. "Same goes."

The other man's eyes narrowed. "Don't tell me Saybrook's is thinking of expanding again?"

The mention of the Trillium Island resort had Ree confused.

"Saybrook's?" She turned her questioning gaze to Dane.

He spread his hands, the very hands that had just been helping to rid her of her clothing. Why, she wondered, did he suddenly look so guilty?

"Ree—"

Townsend was only too happy to fill in the blanks Dane had left so damnably empty. "Didn't Dane mention that he and his sisters own Saybrook's? They've done a lot of developing on the island since acquiring the old resort a few years back. And here you told me you didn't care for developers."

"Developer? You're a developer?" Her voice rose, pushed up a number of decibels by sheer disbelief. This couldn't be happening. It just couldn't be, she told herself. And yet hadn't she thought Dane Conlan too good to be true? Hadn't she felt that her reaction to him was not to be trusted?

"It's not like that."

"Come on, Dane. Don't be so modest," Townsend interjected. Turning to Ree, he said, "The Conlans managed to muck up a sweet little deal I had going to buy Saybrook's. Thanks to an infusion of cash from Luke Banning, they even managed to expand with a golf course on property I had my eye on as well. It looks like he beat me to the finish line here, too. In more ways than one," Townsend murmured, his gaze lingering on Ree's heaving chest.

"Shut up," Dane snapped.

Ree's ears were buzzing, and her stomach felt queasy. "Is…is this true?"

"Not quite the way he says it. You know as well as I do that Townsend is a liar."

The other man shrugged. "What am I lying about? The golf course should be open for business, when, Dane? Late this season or are you waiting till the spring?"

"Spring," Dane said between gritted teeth. He held his bandaged hand out to Regina. "He's making it sound more sinister than it is. He's a master at manipulating a situation to his advantage. I'm not after your property, Ree. You have to believe that. My showing up here was purely accidental."

She relaxed a bit. That was true enough. He hadn't manufactured a boating accident or the injuries he'd suffered. She would give him the chance to explain.

But then Bradley Townsend had her feeling poleaxed all over again when he said, "That kiss didn't look very *accidental*. I wonder what your fiancée would say, Dane?"

The breath hissed out from between Ree's teeth. *"You're engaged?"*

"No. Julie's not my fianceé."

"Julie?" Ree blinked slowly. "So, the woman you are *not* engaged to is named Julie?"

"Can we talk about this another time?" he asked, glancing meaningfully in Bradley's direction. "I would rather explain everything in private."

Ree wanted to let him explain, just as she found herself wanting to believe whatever explanation he offered. But she'd had a lifetime of disappointment from men. Part of her had known she shouldn't have expected more from someone she'd known mere hours. Whether or not this Julie was his fiancée, he obviously knew her well. Yet last night Dane had not mentioned her or any relationship for that matter. Guilt nipped her, since Regina had left out some of the more pertinent details of her personal life as well.

"Whatever you consider Julie Weston after— what?—a few years of dating, she's on the dock with your sisters," Townsend said, only too eager to pour salt in the wounds he'd helped open. "I saw them on my way through town. They were all looking very concerned. Word around town is you've been missing all night." He shook his head and made a tsking sound. "And to think you've been here all the while, passing the time…most comfortably."

Dane ignored Townsend. "Ree, can we talk about this in private. *Please*."

She shook her head. No amount of talking would change the fact that neither one of them was free to pursue whatever it was the obnoxious developer had interrupted.

She never thought she would be grateful for Bradley Townsend's inconsiderate habit of showing up on her doorstep uninvited, but she was glad he had on this day. Things couldn't progress with Dane. She had no business kissing him like that. She had no business wanting to do so much more. That kind of recklessness had doomed her mother and broken her grandparents' hearts.

"I think you should go. Both of you. Now," Ree said quietly. "Maybe Mr. Townsend will be kind enough to give you a lift back to town or let you borrow his cell phone to call your family."

"That's it?" Dane's expression reflected the incredulity in his tone. "You're not going to give me a chance to tell my side of the story?"

She ignored his question. If he issued an explanation she would feel honor-bound to offer one as well. But what purpose would explanations serve at this point? Ree told herself she was being pragmatic rather than acting cowardly.

"Your clothes are hanging in the laundry room. They should be dry by now." She pointed toward the door just off the kitchen. "Goodbye, Dane."

Dane watched her leave. He had more pride than to go after her, especially with Townsend enjoying a ringside seat to his humiliation, and so he went in search of his clothing instead.

No one was in the kitchen when he returned wearing

the stiff, stained and ripped garments he'd had on the day before. He found a pen on the countertop and scribbled a message on the back of her electric bill, which he noted was damned close to being past due.

"Thanks for everything. I'll be in touch and we will discuss this. Dane."

He would call her later. They would get this matter straightened out and put behind them. Surely she would listen to reason once she'd had a chance to cool down.

In the driveway, Townsend was leaning against his Mercedes, his arms folded and his smile several degrees beyond smug.

"I've got to say, Conlan, you've looked better."

Unlike Dane's bedraggled appearance, Bradley's clothes were spotless and neatly pressed. The guy always looked as if he'd stepped off the deck of a yacht.

"Go to hell," Dane muttered.

"Is that anyway to speak to the man who's offering you a ride? Unless you'd rather walk back to town." He snickered and his gaze dropped to Dane's bare feet.

"Yeah, I'd rather walk."

"Suit yourself." Bradley opened the Mercedes's door, but then turned. "By the way, I want to thank you. I wasn't getting anywhere with Regina, but obviously the woman has a soft side. Maybe I've used the wrong approach in my negotiations."

Dane swallowed the worst of his rage. "Like she would be interested in scum like you."

"Ali was."

"Ali was just trying to make Luke jealous. They're happily married now, as you know."

Bradley's smile turned brittle for a moment before he shrugged negligently. "Well, Regina's marriage apparently isn't so happy or she wouldn't have been considering an affair with you."

"M-marriage?" Dane stuttered, too shocked by that verbal bombshell to even consider masking his surprise. "What are you talking about?"

Townsend's expression turned gleeful. "I take it she didn't mention her husband."

Dane thought he'd been battered after being tossed around by story-tall waves the evening before, but that was nothing compared to the way he felt right now.

Glancing back at the house, he thought he caught a glimpse of movement in the stained glass on the front door. Had it really been only a dozen hours ago that he'd knocked on that door to have it swung wide by a gun-toting, dark-haired beauty? The weapon had been a shock, but it was Townsend's claim about her marital status that leveled Dane now.

He had to be wrong.

"Ree's not married."

Townsend started his car. Over its engine's throaty growl Dane could hear his laughter.

"She didn't mention that, huh? Well, according to my sources, she is. See you around, Conlan."

He sped off in a shower of gravel that had Dane hopping back to keep from being pelted. Not that it mattered. He'd already been knocked for a loop.

Regina Bellini was taken? She was off limits?

Anger came then, swift and lethal. She certainly hadn't *kissed* like a woman who had already exchanged vows. She certainly hadn't stopped him when he'd unhooked her bra or tried to remove her shirt.

Hell, no. Her hands had been right there helping his, her breathing just as ragged, her need just as raging and urgent. Then she'd had the nerve to act all aggrieved when she'd learned that Dane had a girlfriend. And, damn her, but he had felt guilty. With this very notable exception, all his dealings with the opposite sex had been based on mutual respect and honesty.

And, when it came to married women, honor. He certainly wouldn't have had his hands all over her if he'd known she had a husband.

As Dane limped off in the direction of the nearest neighbor, he cursed Regina Bellini to perdition again. He didn't care to be played any more than he cared to be made a fool of—and in front of Bradley Townsend of all people. The only bright spot he could see was that once he returned to Trillium, he wasn't likely to run into her again.

Out of sight, out of mind.

CHAPTER FOUR

DANE had a million things to occupy his time, yet he sat at his desk staring out the window at the overcast sky. At least it wasn't raining. The remainder of July and the better part of August had been unseasonably cool and wet—bad news for the resort's bookings but a boon for its newly seeded golf course. It was still too soon for play, but guests had been allowed to take electric-powered carts along the black-topped paths for a tantalizing preview of what the following season at Saybrook's would have to offer.

He was proud of what he, his sisters and Luke Banning had accomplished in such a short time. Already, Saybrook's newly restored resort and soon-to-open Rebel Golf Course had been featured in newspaper articles and golfing magazines from coast to coast.

The buzz was bringing a lot of tourist traffic now that the weather had finally cleared, and that brought more work, none of which he minded. In fact, Dane welcomed the harried pace. Part of the reason he'd gladly worked himself to exhaustion for the past several weeks was he was trying to forget. Even busy, though, Regina Bellini haunted his thoughts.

Out of sight, out of mind? Hell, no. Not Ree. Although Dane felt as if he was going out of his mind, burning up with need each night as he laid awake in his bed and remembered the way she'd felt in his arms.

He'd been attracted to other women before. So, what was it about this one that made her so damned impossible to erase from his memory?

It was her sheer nerve, he decided, taking a sip from his tepid coffee. A couple of the maple trees snagged his attention outside the window. They were already starting to fire up, even though the official start of fall was weeks away. Their bright color reminded him of the lightning show the night of his accident. Nerve, he thought again. Regina had it in spades. Not the kind it took to hoist a shotgun and threaten his life. Uh-uh. The kind it took to kiss him with such contagious passion while conveniently forgetting to mention she had a husband.

He was scowling when Ali poked her head around the door to his office after a brisk knock.

"Hey, Dane."

"What now?" he snapped.

"Something wrong?" Her brow puckered at his harsh tone and he instantly felt contrite. He wasn't one to take out his irritation on others. Generally speaking, he wasn't a moody person, although he had been lately, a fact both his sisters had commented on.

He blew out a breath and shook his head. "Sorry, Al. A lot on my mind."

"I've noticed."

Yet, bless her heart, even now she didn't pry. Audra, he knew, wouldn't let him off the hook so easily. He was thankful she was so busy with Lamaze classes and furnishing a nursery that she didn't have the time to grill him about his breakup with Julie or his overall surliness following his accident.

"What can I do for you?" he asked in a more civil tone, throwing in a smile for good measure.

"Someone's here to see you."

It took an effort not to groan. Today was the official start of the long Labor Day weekend. The resort was packed with down-staters, other affluent guests from around the Midwest and even some East Coasters eager for one last getaway before the school year started back up in earnest and the weather began to turn inhospitable again.

"I don't have any appointments scheduled."

He had purposely left his afternoon free. He had a stack of paperwork that needed to be finished and postmarked before the end of the business day. He didn't want to be interrupted. "Who is it?"

"I don't know." Ali came fully into the room now, closing the door behind her. "She wouldn't give her name, but she said she knew you. She looks…well, nervous for some reason."

It couldn't be, Dane thought. Not here. Not now. And yet, he heard himself ask, "Long, dark hair, a little on the wavy side?"

Ali nodded.

"Thirtyish?"

"Uh-huh. And very attractive."

Killer legs? But Dane kept that question to himself. "Send her in."

He stood as Ali left, an unpalatable blend of anger and curiosity pushing him to his feet. And then Regina Bellini walked into his office and he swore that even from across the room he could smell the subtle scent of her perfume and feel the heat from her skin.

She looked as lovely as he remembered: The heart-shaped face, the tumble of dark hair which she'd tamed with a clip, the nicely proportioned figure. Had she finally come to apologize? To offer some explanation for her completely outrageous behavior? It was galling, but Dane wanted her to. Even more galling, though, was that he still wanted *her*. Just looking at her, he felt it, that low tug and potent punch that he should have been well rid of by now considering how hard he had tried to exorcise it through dogged work by day and long runs along the beach each night.

"Hello, Dane."

He unclenched his jaw long enough to nod and say, "Regina."

She smiled, but he didn't return it. Instead Dane came around his desk and leaned negligently against its edge. All the while, his heart tripped like a jackhammer.

"What brings you here?"

"I…" Her voice trailed off and she glanced away. When she looked at him again, though, she reminded him of the woman who had been so adamant about protecting her property when they first met. The same steely determination flecked her dark gaze. "I'm here on business," she said and he swore her small chin jutted out in challenge.

In stark contrast to the passion and heat that had bubbled to the surface during their last encounter, though, her voice was cool and controlled as she spoke now. Even so, he detected nerves in the way she moistened her lips.

"Business. Is that so?"

"Yes. I have a proposition for you."

The word ricocheted around in his libido for a moment before it registered that she was dressed for success in a slim-fitting black power suit whose skirt hem ended just above her knees. In place of the gun, she held a briefcase.

"Well, then, you should have made an appointment," he replied.

"I would have, but, under the circumstances, I wasn't sure you would have agreed to see me."

"You would have been right."

As he spoke, she worried her lush bottom lip, the same lip he'd once nipped with his teeth. Dane was more than annoyed to find his imagination hadn't embellished the attraction. He'd managed to convince himself during the past several weeks that the sizzle he felt during his time with Ree hadn't been as intense as his memory had made it out to be. Or, if it had been, it likely was the result of his near-death experience and the knot on his head.

His head was fine now. But as she stood within arm's reach of him, looking spit-polished and professional, he still wanted her. He still wanted a *married* woman. Knowing that, he resented her all the more.

"Well, I'm here now," she said, tilting her head to one side in question.

Needing something to do with his hands, Dane retrieved a fountain pen from the desk blotter behind him and levered it through his fingers, a trick from his accounting days. "And I'm busy."

Ree nodded, her gaze following the pen as it flipped over his knuckles. A pair of slim dark brows rose. "So I see."

Dane's fingers grew still.

"Sorry you wasted a trip over from the mainland, but then you of all people should know that folks don't appreciate uninvited guests just dropping in."

She tucked an errant curl behind one ear and shifted her weight to her other foot. "I'm really sorry for the way things ended that day in my kitchen. After what had gone on between us, I…I was rather surprised to discover you were engaged or seriously involved or whatever term it is that you want to use. I'm afraid I didn't handle the situation very well."

Anger flared so abruptly Dane nearly snapped the pricey pen in two. She still thought she had the corner on acting aggrieved? Well, he was only too happy to disabuse her of that notion right now.

"Then I'm sure you know how I felt when Townsend informed me of your marriage."

It was petty and beneath him, but, damn, if he didn't enjoy the way Regina's mouth fell open in surprise and crimson splotched her cheeks. She recovered quickly enough. Under other circumstances, he might have admired her ability to take a well-deserved clip to the chin and still stand facing him with her shoulders unstooped and her nose tipped up.

"Paul and I—" she began before breaking off mid-sentence. She shook her head then and seemed to reconsider what she had been about to say. Finally she said simply, "I'm sorry I didn't tell you myself."

Dane crossed his arms over his chest. That was it? That was all she was going to say on the subject? She offered no explanation and only a bare-bones apology.

His tone was caustic when he asked, "How far would you have allowed things to get before you remembered you were another man's wife?"

"I'm sorry," she said again. "I wanted to tell you, but then…"

He nodded. "Yeah, *then*."

"Well, what about you? How far would you have let things get before mentioning—what was her name again?—Julie?"

Guilt nipped, but it was anger's bite that he really felt. "It's not the same and you damned well know it. Julie and I were never even engaged."

Like a dog with a bone, though, Ree wasn't giving up. "Well, committed, then. Obviously you're in a serious relationship if everyone, including Bradley Townsend, *thinks* you're headed to the altar."

"It wasn't a relationship recognized by the state and the Church," he snapped. "We were just dating."

She blinked. "Were?"

"That's right. Past tense. It's over," Dane said. "I told her what happened and we decided it was time to end things and move on with our lives. Some of us try to be honest."

"I wasn't being dishonest intentionally," Ree stated quietly.

"Oh? Do you often forget to mention that you're married?"

Ree felt heat flare in her cheeks again. "It wasn't like that."

"What was it like?"

It had been heaven, but how could she tell him that now? How could she explain that she was in a loveless, long-over marriage to a man who preferred uncovering the past to creating a future with her? Surely telling Dane that would only make her appear more pathetic than she already felt.

Paul Ritter didn't love her, and any tender feelings she'd had for him had long since withered and died. After those forbidden kisses with Dane, Ree could admit that she'd never enjoyed that kind of passion with her husband. What exactly did that say about the vows she'd once spoken? What did it say about Ree? She had long believed she was above the temptation that had doomed her mother. Apparently that had only been because she hadn't encountered Dane Conlan. One evening with him and she'd all but begged him to make love to her, the consequences be damned.

She pushed those thoughts away and concentrated instead on the reason she had come. "If you could just spare a few minutes of your time. Please."

He heaved a sigh. "Five minutes. That's all I've got right now."

It wasn't a lot of time, but she hoped to God it would be enough to make Dane Conlan an offer he couldn't refuse. And so without preamble, she said, "I want Saybrook's to buy my grandmother's house and the Peril

Pointe property it sits on, with the understanding that the house cannot be razed."

His brow furrowed and she knew her offer had caught him off guard. She hoped it also had him intrigued.

"Why are you selling?"

"The short answer is that I can't afford the taxes any longer, and I don't want to see it turned into another un-inspired chain resort or batch of cookie-cutter condos." She swallowed hard, embarrassed when tears stung her eyes.

"Townsend?"

Ree nodded. "And half a dozen other developers who have since knocked on my door."

Something akin to sympathy flickered in his gaze, but his tone was implacable when he said, "Saybrook's isn't in the market for more property at the moment."

Ree struggled to remain hopeful. "But will you at least consider it?"

Even though she had known Dane only briefly and he had left out the fact he had a girlfriend, she'd done some research on Saybrook's. It wasn't snooty, as she once had assumed. It was a top-notch resort once again thanks to the Conlans and Luke Banning. Word around town was they didn't believe in cutting corners. They de-livered quality, both in accommodations and in service. If Ree had to let the house go, she wanted it in the hands of someone who would take care of it, maybe even cherish it. She was hoping that the man who had once admired the stately Victorian's quarter-sawed oak banister would do that.

When he said nothing, she decided to change tactics. Forget pleading, now she would deal. "I'll offer it to you for ten percent less than what Townsend Development is offering me," she said.

His brows rose. He was interested she decided, even though he asked blandly, "What would we want with a house on the mainland?"

"I've given that some thought." Lowering herself onto one of the chairs angled in front of his desk, she flipped open her brief case. It had been a graduation gift from her grandparents, but today was the first chance she'd had to actually use it. She hoped that was a good omen. Pulling out a file, she held it to Dane, but he didn't reach for it. He glanced meaningfully at his watch instead.

"Summarize it for me."

"Okay. I've done a little research on your resort and the services and amenities you offer your guests. I think you could turn my home into a high-quality, high-demand bed-and-breakfast with a private beach. I was thinking you could call it something like Saybrook's on the Pointe."

If Dane's interest was piqued by her proposal, it didn't show. He looked…bored.

"We specialize in the unique. There are dozens of Victorian bed-and-breakfasts in town."

"None with my view. You said so yourself," she persisted.

"Yes. Over breakfast."

Ree felt her color rise at the reminder, but she moistened her lips and plowed ahead. "You could offer high tea."

"We do that here in Saybrook's dining room."

"The property is prime real estate. It's…it's prime real estate," she repeated, running out of arguments.

Dane straightened and she knew the meeting was over even before he walked to the door and opened it for her. "I'll run it by my sisters and Luke and get back to you."

She wanted to merely nod and walk out, keeping some of her pride, but desperation forced her to ask: "When do you think that might be?"

He shrugged. "We're a little busy right now. A month, give or take."

"I need an answer sooner than that." She cleared her throat. "My taxes are due…soon."

"That's not my problem."

Regina sucked in a breath and expelled it slowly. "No. It's not your problem," she agreed. "It's mine. Well, thank you for your time."

After she'd gone, Dane closed his eyes and slumped against the doorjamb. He'd thought it would feel good to be the one yanking the rug out from under her feet this time. Why did he feel like he was the one who'd just landed on his rear?

Then matters got even more complicated when he opened his eyes to find his sisters standing in the hallway staring at him.

"Who was that?" Audra asked.

He straightened and on a shrug, said, "No one of importance."

"What did she want?" This from Ali.

"Nothing."

"Hmm. Let me see if I've got this straight," Audra tapped one neatly manicured finger against her lips. "No one of importance stopped by for nothing."

"That's right," he snapped.

"And yet you still have your boxers in a knot. Very interesting."

"Let it go, Aud," he warned softly.

She merely grinned. "Let *what* go, big brother?"

Dane walked back into his office on a curse. "I've got work to do," he said before closing the door on his sisters' smiling faces.

Dane didn't want to think about Ree, but he stewed over her and her dilemma for the remainder of the afternoon.

Not my problem, he'd told her, and it wasn't. But it might be good business. That's the only reason he was thinking about her offer, he assured himself. It had nothing to do with the fact that she'd looked so damned desperate and heartbroken when she'd left.

So that evening he invited his sisters and their husbands over for an impromptu barbecue. They were just finishing up a platter of ribs when he mentioned Ree's proposition.

After he outlined the particulars of the deal, Audra asked, "So Nobody of Importance wants us to buy her house?"

Dane sighed heavily. There would be no living down that one. "Yes. Regina Bellini wants Saybrook's to purchase her Victorian and the surrounding acreage."

"I don't get it," Seth piped up. "Why would she think you guys would be interested in buying a house, especially one on the mainland?"

Although Audra's husband wasn't an actual partner in the resort, Dane valued the man's insights. Unfortunately the way he was eyeing Dane right now had him worried that his brother-in-law might see a little too much.

"Expansion, I guess. We're landlocked on Trillium."

"Saybrook's on the Pointe," Ali murmured and glanced up from the proposal Ree had left behind. Dane had made copies of it for everyone. "She put some real thought into this. You'll notice that on page seven she lists possible ways for us to tie in both locations by offering golf course packages and even running a private ferry from a dock on the property."

"Yes, but I still don't understand why she came to us," Audra said, picking up where her husband left off. "More specifically, why did she come to *you?*"

"Saybrook's has a good reputation," Dane evaded. When Audra just kept watching him, he decided to redirect the conversation. "As you can see from the photographs, the property is right on the water. Prime real estate," he added, recalling how Ree had told him that herself. Twice. The words were superfluous then and they were now. Everything on Lake Michigan's coast was prime.

"Where exactly is this?" Luke wanted to know.

"North of the main ferry dock in Petoskey. A few miles, give or take." Despite his vague reply, Dane saw the light dawn in his friend's eyes.

"Good God! She's the one. *Regina Bellini* was your rescuer!"

All hell broke loose then, with his sisters peppering Dane with questions until he thought his head would explode.

"No fair." Seth shouted to be heard over the din. "I didn't get a chance to see her. What does she look like?"

"Let's see," Audra began. "I think the word gorgeous might be a fair assessment."

"I was thinking sexy," Ali added.

"And built." That description earned Luke a good poke in the side from his bride.

"It's interesting that you never mentioned what a little hottie your Good Samaritan is," Audra teased. "For some reason I got the impression that the woman who took you in for the night and tended to your wounds was some babushka-wearing granny decked out in support hose and bifocals."

Dane caught his sisters exchanging glances, no doubt they were now tying the timing of his breakup with Julie to the night he'd spent with Regina and recalling just how surly his mood had been ever since.

"I never mentioned her looks because they aren't important."

"Right," Audra snorted.

"Uh-huh," Ali seconded.

"Drop it guys. She's married."

Four sets of eyes rounded.

"Married?" Audra blinked. "Gosh, honey, I'm sorry."

Dane shoved his chair back from the table and carried his plate over to the sink. "Why the hell are you sorry? She's married. What's the big deal? There's nothing to be sorry about."

"Nothing?" Ali asked.

"Nothing. Not. A. Damned. Thing," he stressed, scraping the food scraps from his dinner plate into the garbage disposal.

He figured the subject was settled. The room had

grown quiet. The only sound was the clinking of dishes and stemware as the table was cleared. Thankfully it appeared his sisters' curiosity had been satisfied.

But then Seth reopened the can of worms. "So, if she has a husband, why did she come to you for help?"

All eyes were on Dane again. He turned on the disposal to give himself a minute to think. Then, he said, "Who knows? Maybe she figures I owe her a favor."

It niggled a bit that he felt that way, too. She might've been a liar, but she'd put a roof over his head and food in his belly. She'd patched up his hand. She'd given him her bed…he'd had a hard time sleeping ever since.

"That's good enough for me," Audra said.

Their partnership in Saybrook's had been her idea, and she could take credit for the massive remodeling efforts throughout the resort. She had a keen knack for business, it turned out. It pleased Dane to see her finally living up to her potential and using the brain God had tucked inside her pretty head, which was why her emotional reaction surprised him.

"This is business, Aud."

"Fine. I'll buy it then. Personally."

Audra was wealthy enough to do just that. She could whip out her checkbook and write out any sum Ree asked and that would be the end of it. Problem solved.

Or would it be? Something told Dane that Regina Bellini would continue to haunt his peace no matter where she lived…or with whom.

Maybe that was why his tone was so impatient when he said, "What would you do with another house, Aud? You and Seth just built one."

"She took care of you, Dane. Who knows what would have happened if she hadn't opened her home to you that night. That's worth the purchase price right there."

"I agree," Ali said.

His sisters regarded him knowingly. He'd shared only the most basic details of his misadventure with his family, downplaying its seriousness. What point was there in scaring them after the fact, especially with Audra pregnant? But they had taken one look at his battered clothing and bruised body and they had known perfectly well how close they'd come to losing him.

"Lakefront property is a good investment," Luke added. He would know, of course, having made much of his vast fortune in real estate. "I might be interested in it myself if we decide to pass on it for the resort."

They discussed the details for another hour. Before his family left, one thing had been decided: They wanted to meet with Ree.

Dane called her as he sat on the end of his dock watching the sun set on Lake Michigan. He held a cordless phone in one hand and a long-necked bottle of beer in the other. Minus the phone, it was the way he unwound most summer evenings, after his run, weather allowing. But he felt keyed up now as he punched in Ree's number and waited for her to answer.

"Hello?"

Just the sound of her voice sent his blood pumping. And so he said tersely, "Keep next Tuesday free. We'd like to tour the property before making any decisions."

He thought he heard her exhale sharply and there was

no mistaking the emotion in her tone when she replied, "I don't know how to thank you."

"No need to thank me. It's business," he said. "You have something I'm interested in, Ree."

After he hung up, the truth of those words teased him late into the night.

CHAPTER FIVE

REE angled the chairs a little more toward the fireplace, stood back to look, sighed and repositioned them again. She had less than an hour before the Conlans and Luke Banning arrived and the fate of her home was decided. Keeping busy hadn't kept her mind off that fact, but it did have its benefits.

She'd spent the long holiday weekend in a frenzy of cleaning, polishing and waxing. As a result, every surface in the huge old house gleamed. The outside had been tidied as well. She had mowed the vast lawn, sweating off a couple pounds in the process since the temperatures reached into the eighties that day and the only mower that she'd been able to start was a push one, and not of the self-propelled variety, either. Despite the energy-sapping heat, she'd also weeded the flower beds. Not much was left blooming at this point besides sedum and some mums, and she regretted not having more annuals to provide color.

The gardens, however, were the least of her worries when it came to the outside. The paint was peeling on the home's white exterior, the railing that ran around the vast porch was missing half a dozen spindles and some of the floorboards were warped and rotted.

Surely the Conlans, who had bought historic Say- brook's and painstakingly restored the resort to its former splendor, would see past the Victorian's deficien- cies to its undeniable structural beauty.

She still couldn't believe they were coming. When Dane had called the previous Friday, she had fully expected him to say they would be passing on her offer. Instead he'd told her Saybrook's other owners wanted a firsthand look at the premises. Her mood had been swinging between relief and trepidation ever since.

With five minutes to go, she steeped tea in her grand- mother's silver service and arranged china cups on a matching polished tray, which she set on a table in the front parlor. She didn't figure Dane was much of a tea drinker, but she was going for effect, setting the stage, and hoping to show her guests what was possible.

When the doorbell chimed, she smoothed down the front of her dress. She'd gone for something floral, with a full skirt and capped sleeves, deciding the rigid lines of her one and only power suit wouldn't serve her well today. Checking her appearance one last time in the foyer mirror, she opened the door with a smile affixed on her face.

Dane stood on the porch. The last time they had faced one another over the threshold, he'd been drenched to the skin, his clothing torn and soiled. On this day, he wore a snowy-white shirt tucked into a pair of tailored dark trousers. His tie was loosened, the cuffs of his sleeves rolled up as if he were eager to get down to business.

"Hello, Ree."

"Hello."

She stepped back, but he didn't come inside. Instead he crossed to one of the padded wicker chairs on the porch. "The others should be along anytime. They stopped in town. Audra had to, um, use a restroom."

"I hear that's common for pregnant women."

He made a dismissive noise. "I wouldn't know."

She settled into the chair next to his. "Me, either."

Dane motioned toward the door. "Will anyone else be joining us today?"

"No. I...I didn't think to hire a lawyer or real estate agent to represent me in the sale."

"That's not who I meant," he said.

"Who else would I invite?" she asked, baffled.

Dane just shook his head. "Never mind."

Another vehicle pulled up the driveway a moment later, thankfully interrupting the awkward silence. Introductions were made.

"This is Ali Banning. She's a partner in Conlan Development."

"I'm also his sister," the slender brunette said on a wink. "We met the day you came to the resort, although I didn't catch your name then and I didn't realize you were the one who had taken such good care of my brother after his accident."

"Oh." She flushed, unsure how to respond, especially since Dane was scowling. "It's a pleasure to meet you, Mrs. Banning."

"It's just Ali, please. And the pleasure is mine. Thank you for what you did for Dane."

"It was no trouble," she replied awkwardly.

"This is my husband, Luke, and my sister, Audra Ridley."

"I'll add my thanks to Ali's. We're very grateful for what you did," Audra said.

"Give it a rest," Ree thought she heard Dane mutter under his breath.

"By the way, vanity requires that I make sure you know I'm pregnant, not fat."

Even with her abdomen rounded with child, she was still one of the most striking and fashionable women Ree had ever encountered.

"I love your shoes," she found herself saying as she eyed the pointy-toed flats. She hadn't had the opportunity to shop much in the past several years, but that didn't mean she didn't know what she liked. "Italian, right?"

"Of course. Great, aren't they?" Audra pursed her lips then. "They're a little tight these days. I've heard rumors that your feet grow with childbirth. I'm praying to God that's not so."

"And I'm praying it is," Ali said on a smirk. Holding out one foot, she added, "We're the same size. At least we were."

"As enlightening as I find this topic, we're not here to discuss footwear," Dane interrupted.

Even though his impatient tone had the sisters glancing over sharply Ree knew he was right.

"I want to thank you all for coming. I know you're busy businesspeople and I really appreciate your taking time out of your schedule today," she said. Her hands had begun to shake, and so she clasped them in front of her. "I have refreshments inside or I can show you around the grounds first."

"Let's go with the grand tour," Audra said with a wink. "Once I sit down, it's hard for me to get back up."

They walked the perimeter of the house. Despite Ree's best efforts, nothing could hide the obvious neglect, so she tried to draw their eyes away from it and have them focus instead on the home's finer points.

"There are several styles of Victorian—Gothic Revival, Italianate, Romanesque, to name just a few. This one is actually a Queen Anne, which is probably the most popular of the designs and the one that comes readily to mind when people think of Victorian architecture."

She pointed to the gingerbread trim and stained-glass windows that reflected the afternoon sun.

"Queen Anne's are known for their excessive use of adornment and decoration. You'll notice the patterned brickwork on the chimneys and the detailed shingle design over the eyebrow dormer and on the outside of the tower."

"You seem to know a lot about Victorian architecture," Ali said.

Her grin was sheepish. "Actually I went to the library over the weekend and read up on it. I wanted to be prepared for your visit."

"It shows," Luke said. "And we appreciate it. Right, Dane?"

Dane merely shrugged.

"Wow. Talk about an incredible view." Audra said and meandered toward the beach, one hand supporting the underside of her belly. The rest of them followed.

"It's gorgeous," Ali seconded.

Waves crested white on the lake's sapphire surface. Far out, Ree could just make out the silhouette of a freighter that was heading in the direction of the Straits of Mackinac.

"I see lots of potential here. I can picture a boardwalk, lantern lighting, maybe even a string quartet set up over there to provide music on summer evenings." Ali pointed to where the high grass that shot up from the dunes waved in the breeze.

"Dancing under the stars," Audra mused. "Oh, and just look at that gazebo. It doesn't look very old."

"It's not, relatively speaking. My grandparents had it built when I was in grade school."

They walked there next.

"I bet you spent a lot of time here as a girl," Audra said, stepping up into the multisided structure. Benches lined the inside walls, each one padded with pillows whose floral print was now faded and stained.

"Yes, I did," she said, lost in the memory. "I used to pretend it was a lighthouse and I was the beacon's keeper, helping those who were lost find their way home."

Of course, the person she'd hoped to steer home had never returned. But someone else had found his way to her door.

Dane's gaze tangled with her for a moment before he looked away. Then he frowned. "Is that a stone cross over there?"

"Marble, actually." And imported from her grandparents' native Italy. "It…it can come down, of course. It's a memorial."

"For whom?" Ali asked.

Dane answered before Regina could. "Your mother?"

"Yes." For the others' benefit, she added, "She died when I was six."

Dane's gaze turned soft with understanding. "She died here, didn't she."

Ree eyed the tall marker that had stood a dozen yards up from the highwater mark on the beach for more than twenty years. It was weathered now having been battered by ice and rain and baked in the hot summer sun. But she could still recall how shiny and cool the marble had felt under her hands the day her grandparents had had it installed on the first anniversary of their daughter's death.

"Yes. She drowned." And in her mind's eye she watched Angela Bellini walk purposefully into the surf and disappear beneath the waves.

"How awful," Audra said.

"That had to be hard for you," Ali added.

Luke, who'd known his own share of tragedy as a child, murmured a soft, "I'm sorry."

As Dane watched, though, Ree shrugged off his family's condolences.

"It was a long time ago," she said. Yet he didn't get the feeling that made the loss any easier to accept.

For the first time since arriving on her doorstep that day, he allowed himself to consider how hard this meeting had to be for her. This was her home. It held all of her memories, good and bad. And she was selling it. She would be leaving it to live somewhere else.

He touched her arm. The contact was fleeting but

intended to offer comfort. She turned in surprise and something flickered briefly in those dark eyes that had beguiled him from the first. Gratitude, he told himself. That's all he saw. He didn't have a right to want to see anything more.

"Why don't you show us the inside now," he said.

For the next forty-five minutes, Ree led them on a room-by-room tour. Several of the upstairs bedrooms were not furnished, but the hardwood floors were polished and the corners were free of cobwebs. She kept a clean house, and a homey one. That much he remembered from before. But on this day Dane found himself glancing around, looking beyond the doilies and knickknacks of the front parlor for signs of the man Ree was married to. He spied none. Not so much as a sports magazine or pair of work boots or a framed photograph.

Even in the bedroom where Dane had awoken to sunshine the morning after near-tragedy—the bedroom that Ree had said was hers—he spotted nothing particularly masculine. And he looked, scanning the top of the dresser for cuff links or other small clues he might have missed the last time, and glancing inside the closet after Ali opened it. Only women's clothing hung inside. He attributed his interest to basic curiosity. It was only natural to wonder about a man whose wife chose not to use his last name, a man who did not share his wife's home. Something here didn't add up.

His sisters apparently noticed that, too.

"Dane tells us you're married," Audra said conversationally as they walked back to front parlor. "Will your husband be joining us today?"

Ree's gaze slid to Dane before she busied herself at the tea service. "No. Paul is away on business."

"Oh? What does he do?" Luke inquired.

"He's an archaeologist. He's on a dig right now in the Nevada desert, I believe."

"That sounds exciting. Do you ever accompany him?" Audra asked.

"I used to, but I…I don't any longer."

"And he trusts you to stay home alone?" Dane's words carried such obvious insult that his sisters glanced sharply in his direction. Even Luke raised his eyebrows in question.

Ree wasn't cowed, though. For the first time all afternoon, real color rose in her pale cheeks. "Trust is a two-way street," she replied, giving as good as she got.

"Um, so, your husband must be okay with the sale," Audra commented.

"The property is mine to do with what I wish. My grandmother left it to me exclusively in her will. Paul has no claim on it."

Her stark words were at odds with Dane's definition of marriage, but he kept that thought to himself. He was already in the doghouse with his sisters thanks to his last stinging remark.

After a moment, Ree excused herself on the pretext of reheating the tea, but Dane figured she wanted to give them time alone to discuss the property.

"Well, I love this place," Audra announced the moment Ree was out of earshot. "I was all for buying it sight unseen. Now, having seen it, I'm even more convinced that this would be a sound investment and a wonderful addition to Saybrook's."

Luke and Ali chimed in then, offering their views, which were pretty much in line with Audra's. Then Ali poked Dane in the ribs, "So, what's going on between you and Regina Bellini anyway?"

"Nothing."

"Right," Audra said dryly. "And I'm not pregnant."

"Okay, when we first met, she didn't divulge…some key facts," he hedged.

"Key facts," Audra mused. "Well, don't stop there. You've got me curious."

"The, um, withholding of those key facts resulted in a…misunderstanding and some hard feelings."

"Well, get over it already," Ali advised, earning a shout of laughter from her husband.

"This from the woman who carried a grudge against me for more than a decade."

"That was different, Luke. I loved you and you broke my heart."

Three sets of eyes snapped back to Dane, and he would have had to be blind to miss the speculation.

Dane was the last to leave Regina's home. He told himself it was only because Luke's Cadillac was parked behind his Trailblazer, but he had a couple questions he wanted answered. Once they were alone, he asked the one that seemed the least damning.

"So, what are you going to do now?"

"Tonight?"

"Actually I was speaking in more general terms," he clarified. "For all intents and purposes, your house is sold. We're giving you your asking price. Assuming there are no sizable liens on the property, you can go anywhere, do anything. Not that it's any of my business, but I was wondering what that might be."

"Oh. I'm not sure."

She blew out a breath and gathered the heavy cascade of hair into a rope at the base of her neck before letting it loose again. The absent gesture still had his groin going tight. All day he'd told himself that he was over the non-sensical attraction he'd felt for her. Over it. Yet now that they were alone, the sensation washed over him again, and Dane felt as helpless as he had bobbing around in Lake Michigan, pulled by forces beyond his control.

She was still speaking he realized, something about going to Italy.

"My grandparents are buried there now and I'd like to make sure the headstones I ordered have been installed. And I need to find a job, of course. Beyond that…" She shrugged.

"Will…will you be joining your husband?" Dane asked quietly. God help him, but he needed to know.

"No. My marriage—"

"Is none of my business," he interrupted, coming to his senses at last. The woman's private life was just that. Even so, it was difficult to ignore the outrageous relief he felt that Regina Bellini's answer had not been yes.

But Ree didn't let subject close. "Paul and I are legally separated. We have been since I moved back to Michigan to care for Nonna."

"I'm…" Sorry? The word stuck in his throat.

"I know it doesn't excuse my behavior that night. I'm not…I don't…" She blew out a breath. "I've never been like that with anyone else. It's hard to explain."

Not so hard. He understood perfectly.

"You should try to work things out," Dane said at last, forcing aside the more selfish urge to advise her differently. But what kind of man would that make him? "Marriage should be forever."

"I know. I wanted it to be, believe me."

"It takes hard work."

Her smile was sad. "That's what Nonna told me."

"Well, you should listen to your grandmother."

"Is that what you…would do?" she asked.

"We're not talking about me." Dane shoved a hand through his hair and paced toward the steps. He intended to leave, but he found himself turning around instead.

"I have an offer for you."

The words came as a surprise, even though he supposed the germ of this idea had been festering since she'd walked them through the Victorian, pointing out its finer features. He didn't want to think that the revelation she'd just made about her marriage had anything to do with what he was about to say.

"What kind of an offer?"

"Employment," he said, succinctly and with determination. Yet he stumbled over the words when he added, "I want you…I want you to oversee the renovations."

Ree blinked in surprise. "That could take months."

"I'm aware of that. You said you needed a job. I'm giving you one."

"What will your sisters and Luke think about that?"

"It was their idea," he lied smoothly. Surely his sisters would have suggested it had they thought of it earlier, eager as they were to repay Regina for her kindness.

"I see." Still, she tilted her head to one side, regarding him warily. "Why?"

He took a step back, tucked his hands into the front pockets of his trousers. He didn't want to more closely examine his motives, so his tone was gruff when he said, "If you're not interested, just say so."

"Oh, I'm interested." He swore she blushed then. Or maybe his ego just needed to believe she felt as flustered and awkward as he did. "I just…don't understand why you all would be willing to do this for me. I'm hardly an expert on renovations or even Victorian architecture."

"You impressed my sisters and Luke as being a quick study."

"So this isn't charity?"

"We're in business for profit," Dane replied dryly. "You'll have to earn your keep."

Of course, there was one little side bonus. Having Ree close at hand while knowing she was off-limits was bound to help exorcise these lingering feelings he had for her. Once he got to know her better, once he discovered all her idiosyncrasies and annoying habits, this white-hot awareness would burn itself out.

"The place needs a complete facelift inside and out to be up to Saybrook's standards." He chipped some paint off the weathered porch rail for emphasis. "You know what it used to look like, I assume."

She nodded. "I even have pictures that the previous

owners left my grandparents. They're black and white, but they should be helpful."

"Good. Come by my office later this week. We'll go over the terms of your employment and determine the appropriate compensation."

"Can I…can I live here during the work?"

"Are you sure you want to do that? Contractors will be walking in and out, making all sorts of noise and creating all sorts of messes."

Ree shrugged. "If it gets too crazy I'll make other arrangements, but I'd really like to stay on the premises."

"Okay, we'll save your bedroom for last."

Her face brightened and a hint of a smile began to turn up the corners of her mouth. His own went dry. "Thanks, Dane. You don't know how much I appreciate this."

The gratitude he saw made him uncomfortable and, oddly, a little angry. He didn't want her damned gratitude. He wanted something he couldn't have, something he was wrong to even consider.

"Thank my sisters," he said.

Ree waited until the Trailblazer turned onto the main road before she twirled around in a circle and settled happily onto the top step of the porch.

She had a job and a home for the time being, her two most pressing problems taken care of in one fell swoop. The Conlans had seen to that. Even with things so strained between them, Dane had reached out in kindness. It was business, he'd said. And it was indeed that. But it was also humane. Her respect for him notched up higher. As did her forbidden attraction. She would have to keep a firm grip on that. The last thing she wanted to do was repay his family's decency and soil what was left of her grandparents' good name by acting on the damnable passion that kept bubbling to the surface no matter how hard she tried to cap it.

CHAPTER SIX

WITH the official tourist season over, the resort's hectic pace slowed considerably, even though summer made a last stand in September with a batch of days in the low eighties.

Dane decided to take a half day off midweek to make some repairs to his dock before he hauled it in for the winter. He'd been expecting Regina at the office. They had an appointment set for ten to go over her responsibilities and compensation. She hadn't showed. Nor had she called. She didn't strike him as the irresponsible sort and unless she was an incredible actress, she had clearly been excited about his offer. Yet there was no sign of her.

He gave up waiting after two hours and headed for home. It was irritation, certainly not worry, that had him checking in with his secretary four times by one o'clock to see if Ree had put in an appearance or left a message.

He was shirtless, his tan cargo shorts wet from standing in waist-deep water, when he heard a vehicle pull up his driveway. He came around the corner of the house in time to see a vintage, bright yellow Volkswagen Beetle pull to a stop. It shouldn't have surprised him that Regina was behind the wheel of an old car that obviously had been well cared for.

"Hello." She smiled brightly. "I stopped by the resort, but Audra said you'd already gone home for the day. She gave me directions and said to come out. I hope you don't mind."

"I was expecting you at ten. It's now, what, two? Do you make it a habit of showing up four hours late for a meeting? If so, maybe the job we're offering you isn't such a good idea."

"I'm sorry." Color had suffused her cheeks only to blanch back out at his last statement. "My car...he's very temperamental. And then I missed the ferry and had to wait another hour."

Dane cocked his head to one side. He couldn't have heard her correctly. "Your car is a he?"

"Yes." She shrugged.

"I suppose you named...him?"

"Oliver," Ree supplied without hesitation. "You know, after the orphan in the Dickens classic. I got Oliver at a government auction."

Dane was angry with her. Yet he found himself wanting to laugh or at least grin. And that ticked him off all the more.

"You could have at least called to let me know you would be late. I remember you saying you have a cell phone."

"Had, actually." Ree raised her chin. "I, um, streamlined my expenses last month."

It was a fancy way of saying she was broke, at least

until the purchase of her home was final. Husband or no husband, her love for the big Victorian notwithstanding, Regina obviously needed the money from that sale and the job Dane had discussed with her last week. He wasn't such a hard case that he could snatch back the opportunity now.

"Give me a minute to drag on some clean clothes," he said gruffly. With that he turned and left.

Ree watched Dane disappear through the side door of the house. He wasn't pleased. Again. And yet she'd sworn she'd seen his lips twitch when they'd discussed her car's gender. Maybe there was hope yet for friendship between them.

Friendship. Was that what she wanted? Was that *all* she wanted? Recalling the way he'd looked just now, shirtless, slim hips hugged by wet cotton, she felt that low, slippery pull of passion. As seductive as it was, it also concerned her. Could it be that despite her best efforts she was just like her mother? Irresponsible and impulsive. Doing what felt good at the moment and ignoring the consequences. Or, was she like her father? A cheat. Doing what felt good and ignoring her commitments.

Hers was quite the pedigree.

Dane Conlan, on the other hand, had plenty of self-control. Indeed even after all that had passed between them in her kitchen, when he'd learned about Paul, he'd told her she should work on her foundering marriage.

She'd long despised her husband's apathetic approach to everything but his work, but was she any better? She could have forced the issue one way or another, taken the final steps to see the marriage ended officially. She'd filed the paperwork, but there had been no follow-through and that hadn't been just for Nonna's sake. Oh, she had taken off her rings and returned to using her maiden name, but those things hardly changed the facts.

She glanced down at her bare fingers now. The rings had gone to a good cause. She'd hocked them the previous winter to help pay for some plumbing repairs. But money wasn't the only reason she'd done it. She still had the diamond ring that had belonged to her grandmother. No matter how tight things had gotten, she never considered selling it. That ring symbolized something real and enduring, something like the Victorian that could, with care and nurturing, withstand the test of time. Her princess-cut diamond and thick gold band had represented only failure.

Ree walked around to the side of the home that faced the lake and sighed at the view, finding comfort in its beauty. The big lake stretched for miles, its vast surface was calm today beneath a hazy September sky whose mix of blue and gray hues reminded Ree of the color of Dane's eyes.

She heard the door squeak open and turned to find him on the ample covered porch wearing jeans and a polo shirt. He'd combed his dark hair, but he remained shoeless.

"The paperwork is back at the office, but the gist of it is Saybrook's will expect you to put in whatever hours are needed until the project is completed. Your weekends will be your own unless the main contractor or a subcontractor absolutely needs to see you."

He rattled off a wage that had her sucking a breath between her teeth.

"Something wrong?"

"No. Nothing. I wasn't expecting…that's very generous. Thank you."

"You'll earn it, believe me. Until I sign off on the renovations, you'll be at my beck and call."

He frowned after he said it.

"Will you be working with me on the project then?" Ree had wondered, since Audra and Ali had been responsible for her hiring, if she would report to his sisters.

"Not exclusively, but Ali and Luke have other responsibilities, mainly the new golf course. And with Audra due to deliver her baby soon, she's not likely to be heavily involved in much of anything for the next several months. So, any questions?"

It was the perfect opening to ask about what she had in mind. Here goes nothing, Ree thought, screwing up her courage. For the past few days she'd been rehearsing how best to put into words the idea that had been kicking around in her head.

"Actually it's not a question as much as it is a…request."

"Oh?"

"I know I'm not really in any position to be making requests."

He gave a curt nod. "I'm glad you understand that."

Ree swallowed hard before continuing. "You're going to need a manager for the bed-and-breakfast once it opens for business, right?"

"Yes."

"I'd like to be considered for the job."

Dane's eyebrows shot up in surprise. "You want to

manage the bed-and-breakfast? I wasn't aware you had a background in hospitality services or business for that matter."

"Actually, I don't. My degree is in journalism. But I'm a hard worker and a fast learner."

"I'll be the judge of that."

She planned to make sure he agreed with her description when it was all said and done. "Please, say you will at least consider me for the job once the bed-and-breakfast opens."

"Ali actually oversees personnel and she might have someone already on the payroll that she thinks is ready for the promotion." His gaze was probing. "But I can make a recommendation if I feel strongly about someone."

"So, I can apply?"

He nodded. "I'll let her know that you're interested and I'll give her an evaluation after renovations are under way. No guarantees, you understand."

She exhaled slowly. "I understand. Thanks."

"Why would you want to work there?"

"I'd get to stay in my home."

Dane said nothing. What words were there in response to that? The simplicity of her reason touched him deeply given his own strong connection to home and family. And he thought again about how much she had lost. Her mother had drowned just off the point. Her grandparents, who had loved the house, were gone now, too. Letting go of one's childhood home would be difficult under any circumstance, but usually families moved to other homes where new memories could be made. Ree had no family left with whom she could make those memories. No family except an absentee father and an equally estranged husband.

"It must please you to know the Victorian will be restored."

"It does. The house has a fascinating history."

"Oh?"

"Some of it I know from my grandmother, but I did a little more research recently, hoping to find information on the structure. Want to hear it?"

"By all means," he said, suckered in by the excitement shimmering in her dark eyes.

"The original owner was Thomas Trent Windamere, who made his fortune in Great Lakes shipping. He had three daughters, whom he named Felicity, Charity and Honor. His wife died in childbirth with the last one. Windamere doted on his girls. They were his life. And so when Charity became ill with a lung ailment, he had this house built on Peril Pointe hoping the fresh air would ease her condition."

"And did it?" Dane asked, intrigued despite himself.

"I don't know. The information I found at the historical society didn't say. I guess I'd like to think she lived a long and happy life."

He shook his head, amazed that she had gone to such lengths to flesh out the home's history.

"Are you always so passionate?" He regretted his choice of words immediately when Ree's face blanched of color.

"I'm…I'm not…" she stammered.

Her reaction surprised him, but he supposed given

what had transpired between them, she would be sensitive to even the most innocuous reminder.

"I didn't mean it as an insult. I just meant that you're thorough and thoughtful. It's like with the proposal you brought with you when you pitched your property to Saybrook's. You think things out very carefully."

"Not everything," she said, staring straight ahead. And Dane thought he knew exactly to what she was referring.

After a few moments of silence, Ree took a deep breath and decided to change the subject, "You have a lovely view. Have you lived here long?"

"I grew up here," Dane said. "My folks moved to Florida a while back, and I bought the house from them. I didn't want strangers buying it and living here, or worse, weekenders trashing the place."

His face grew red as he apparently realized that Ree's home would soon be filled with strangers—paying guests, but strangers nonetheless.

"Sorry," he mumbled.

She waved a hand in his direction. "It's okay. I know what you mean, but the Victorian is different. I think she'll like being a grand lady again, rooms filled with people who will appreciate her beauty."

"She?"

"Everyone knows Victorians are females."

"And Volkswagen Beetles are males."

"Exactly."

He laughed softly and shook his head. "I suppose you've named the house, too."

"No. My grandmother did that. Bella. It's Italian for—"

"Beautiful," he murmured and his gaze lingered on her lips.

The afternoon sun was beating down. She blamed it for the warmth spreading through her limbs.

"Well, I should let you get back to your work," Ree said, nodding toward the dock where his toolbox was open.

"Actually, I was thinking about taking a break. I've got some iced tea. Made it when I got home. It should be good and chilled by now."

"Is that an invitation?"

"Yes."

Ree waited on the porch, tucked into one of the big Adirondack chairs, her feet propped on the matching ottoman. She felt some of the tension of the past several weeks slipping away as she gazed out at the lake. Dragonflies buzzed overhead, zipping erratically in their search for prey. Far on the horizon, she could just make out the white sail of a boat.

Dane returned a moment later with two tall glasses of iced tea.

"It's not sweetened," he told her, as he handed her one.

"Doesn't need to be. I'm an easy woman to please."

One eyebrow cocked up, but he said nothing as he settled into the chair next to hers.

"So, you grew up here with your sisters. That must have been fun."

"Not at the time," he replied on a grunt. "But looking back now, I can say it was. I had a good childhood. Good parents—strict, but loving."

"My grandparents filled that role for me." She drank her tea, recalling the many lazy afternoons she had spent

The Harlequin Reader Service® — Here's how it works:

NO POSTAGE
NECESSARY
IF MAILED
IN THE
UNITED STATES

BUSINESS REPLY MAIL
FIRST-CLASS MAIL   PERMIT NO. 717-003   BUFFALO, NY

POSTAGE WILL BE PAID BY ADDRESSEE

HARLEQUIN READER SERVICE
3010 WALDEN AVE
PO BOX 1867
BUFFALO NY 14240-9952

If offer card is missing write to: Harlequin Reader Service, 3010 Walden Ave., P.O. Box 1867, Buffalo NY 14240-1867

Get FREE BOOKS and a FREE GIFT when you play the...

LAS VEGAS
GAME

*Just scratch off
the gold box with a coin.
Then check below to see
the gifts you get!*

YES! I have scratched off the gold box. Please send me my **2 FREE BOOKS** and **gift for which I qualify**. I understand that I am under no obligation to purchase any books as explained on the back of this card.

▼ DETACH AND MAIL CARD TODAY! ▼

386 HDL EFZP   186 HDL EFYE

FIRST NAME   LAST NAME

ADDRESS

APT.#   CITY

(H-R-08/06)

STATE/PROV.   ZIP/POSTAL CODE

| 7 | 7 | 7 | Worth TWO FREE BOOKS plus a BONUS Mystery Gift! |

Worth TWO FREE BOOKS!

TRY AGAIN!

www.eHarlequin.com

Offer limited to one per household and not valid to current Harlequin Romance® subscribers. All orders subject to approval.

with them in just this way, sipping a cool beverage and talking about any subject that came to mind. "A lot of people are eager to leave the place where they grew up. I never was."

"Audra was hell-bent for leather to get out," Dane told her. "Luke Banning, too. They left at the same time. Together, actually, but that's another story and not nearly as interesting as a lot of folks around here used to make it sound."

"Gossip rarely is."

Her family had been the subject of it more than once. In fact, part of the reason Ree's grandfather had retired early was to take his pregnant and unwed teenage daughter out of the city and away to a remote location where no one knew she'd given in to the charms of an older, married man. Then, after Angela's suicide, the elder Bellinis had had to contend with whispers in their new community.

"Doesn't keep people from spreading it."

"No," she agreed. "Or from embellishing everything. I'd heard of Luke Banning from the newspapers, of course, long before I realized he grew up around these parts. He's highly respected for his business instincts when it comes to real estate. Did you know him when you were kids?"

"Best friends," Dane said.

Something about the way one side of his mouth curved up into a half grin told Ree the men had plenty of good stories to tell, not that either one of them appeared to be indiscreet.

"Audra became an actress, right?"

He nodded. "She never made it big—a couple of sitcom episodes, that sort of thing. But no real starring roles unless you count the melodrama that was her personal life." He spoke the words without malice. In fact, he seemed proud when he added, "She really managed to turn things around after a few false starts."

By "false starts" Ree assumed he was referring to his sister's string of well-publicized bad relationships. Even out on remote dig sites, Ree had heard about them, in part because of an intern's penchant for reading celebrity magazines. With her own marriage in the toilet, Ree was in no position to cast stones, not that she'd ever been terribly judgmental about other folks. How could she be given her family history? Besides, Audra was so obviously smitten now.

"She seems very happy. And I'd say she is lucky. She and Seth are very much in love."

"Sickeningly so," Dane agreed. "She claimed she felt a connection to him right from the beginning."

He frowned then, and Ree wondered if he was recalling the instantaneous attraction that had flared between the pair of them that first night despite a raging storm, a power outage and his assorted injuries. Of course, that was sex, hormones. It wasn't love.

She quickly redirected the conversation. "But you and Ali stayed on Trillium. Ever thought about leaving?"

"Nah. It's home," he said with a shake of his head, his gaze scanning the horizon where the sky meshed seamlessly with the big lake. "I don't just mean this house. I like the island, the people, the slower pace of life around here." He sipped his tea. "Well, slower pace now that most of the fudgies have gone home for the season."

He used the affectionate nickname for the downstaters who came to vacation, often buying fudge at the many shops found sprinkled amid the resort communities of northern Michigan.

Ree chuckled. "I had a job at a fudge shop one summer."

"Get out."

"No, really. On Mackinac Island the summer before I went away to college."

"What? Trillium Island not good enough for you?" he teased. "We have fudge shops."

"Too close to home. I was going to be heading to Michigan State the following fall and I'd never been away from Petoskey for more than a weekend at a time. I decided I needed to test my wings a bit first."

"How'd you do?"

"I was too homesick for words," she admitted on a laugh. "And I gained seven pounds snacking on fudge. Mint was my favorite."

He pulled a face. "Pralines and cream, *maybe* peanut butter, but you'd never catch me eating anything with mint in it. Too…mouthwashy."

"You don't know what you're missing. Have you at least tried it?"

"No need. I know what I like and what I don't." He studied her thoughtfully for a moment, before saying, "Why don't you get back to your story? You were telling me how homesick you were."

"Yes. Very. But I gutted it out and then put on a brave

face when my grandparents dropped me off in East Lansing in August. Nonna, of course, cried. My grandfather was much more stoic, although he kept complaining about seasonal allergies and blowing his nose."

She smiled briefly, the memory so sweet and clear that she could almost feel Nonna's tight embrace and smell the Old Spice aftershave her grandfather had favored. A decade later, they were both gone and she was selling the home they'd poured their retirement savings into.

"It must have been hard for them to watch you go," Dane said.

"It was. Especially since I think they knew I would never really come back. I had internships at downstate newspapers between my sophomore and junior years and again the following summer."

"And then you got married," he said flatly.

Ree cleared her throat. "Yes, I met Paul during my senior year at State. He was just finishing up his doctorate. Our wedding was a few months after I earned my bachelor's degree."

She remembered it all clearly now. They'd met in the campus library, where they'd shared a table. Paul had been so utterly absorbed in his studies that Ree had been seated for nearly an hour before he glanced up and finally noticed her. He'd smiled. She'd smiled back. And, when the library closed that evening, he asked her out. During their courtship, she had found his single-mindedness funny if sometimes frustrating. She'd convinced herself that his ability to focus on one thing to the exclusion of all else was a trait to be admired. What other qualities had drawn her to someone so different from herself, she no longer could remember.

"Is your husband from around here?"

"No. He's from Ohio originally, but he lived in about a dozen states before moving to Michigan to attend MSU. His dad was in the military."

"Nomadic," Dane murmured.

"Yes and he still is."

"His work?"

Ree nodded. "It takes him a lot of places, sometimes for months at a stretch."

Her tone must have turned rueful, because Dane said, "You had to have known that going in, though."

"I did," she agreed. "Well, sort of. Paul had a teaching assistant job at the university when we married and there was the offer of something more permanent, but he wanted to do a couple of years in the field. He promised that after that he'd look for a professorship."

Promises made. Promises broken. Two years had turned into four, four into six and counting. The offers had come. Ree had stopped keeping track after half a dozen. Paul had rejected each one. And, oh, the arguments that had ensued. Ree passionately pleading her case. Paul calmly discounting each point she made when he finally engaged in conversation.

"He must enjoy his work."

"It's his life."

Dane glanced at her sharply, but said nothing for a long moment. When he did speak, it was just one shattering comment.

"You should be his life."

Ree rubbed at the condensation collecting on the outside of her glass. She didn't know why, but she had the sudden urge to cry.

"Well, this is it."

Ree said the words aloud as she pulled into the lot at Saybrook's the first week in October. She shifted the Volkswagen into Park, killed the ignition, and then sat for a moment, staring out at the rain that drizzled from a pewter sky. They were closing on the sale of the house today.

Oddly, the prospect of facing Dane again had her nerves jangling more than the fact that she was about to hand over ownership of her home. The last time they'd seen one another, she'd sworn something had shifted between them. It scared her almost as much as the attraction.

She gathered up her briefcase, got out of the car and, since she didn't have an umbrella, made her way to the resort's entrance as quickly as was prudent in high heels on wet asphalt. The Conlans and Luke already were assembled in Saybrook's conference room with a couple sober-looking, suited men she assumed were lawyers.

"Ree, come in," Ali said after glancing up and spotting her in the doorway. "Can I get you a cup of coffee or some hot tea?" She motioned toward the rain-splattered window. "Nasty out today, huh?"

"Yes. Tea would be great, please."

As she unbuttoned her coat, she spied Dane. He was dressed in a suit as well, his hair tidy and cheeks freshly shaved. Neatly put together or hopelessly disheveled, the man always looked mouthwatering. It wasn't fair.

Ree ran one hand down the wavy length of her hair. She hadn't bothered trying to straighten it today. The weather being what it was, she'd known it would be a wasted effort. Now she regretted that she hadn't at least pulled it back into some sort of professional-looking 'do. For just a moment, she swore she heard Nonna clucking her tongue.

Dane stepped forward to help her out of her overcoat, under which she wore the same suit she'd had on the day she came to Saybrook's to plead her case. He was standing so close, she could smell the clean scent of his aftershave. She inhaled deeply and wanted to sigh.

"Hello, Ree."

"Hi." The one syllable came out embarrassingly breathy. She cleared her throat and redeemed herself with a more normal-sounding, "How are you?"

"Good. What about you? It's a big day."

"Oh, I'm fine." And she meant it. She had accepted that the sale was necessary and inevitable. Even so, she was happy to change the subject. "I have something for you…and the others, too, of course."

She pulled a small white box out of her briefcase and handed it to him. Dane was laughing even before he opened it. "I can't believe you brought me fudge."

"I saw the shop when I got off the ferry and couldn't resist, considering the conversation we had."

"Pralines and cream," he said, nicking a small chunk off the end with his fingers and then plopping it in his mouth. A single dimple winked low in his cheek when he smiled.

"You said it was your favorite." Then Ree produced another small white box.

"What's in that one?" Dane asked.

"Mint." She couldn't help herself. She grinned. "Because you don't know what you've been missing."

He wrinkled his nose. "I'm not a fan of mint."

"So you said the other day, but that's only because you haven't tried it in fudge."

He sighed heavily. "I'll sample it, but don't expect me to be a convert," he warned.

"You need to keep an open mind, Dane. Why limit your choices? You know, sometimes it pays to take risks."

"Risks," he repeated, his voice just above a whisper. For a fleeting moment, heat flared so intensely in his eyes that Ree was forced to glance away. That's when her gaze collided with Audra's, and she realized that Dane's sister had heard the entire conversation. Make that *sisters.* Luke and the lawyers were thankfully embroiled in a conversation of their own, but Dane's siblings had caught Ree's and Dane's every word. While it had hardly been titillating repartee, the look the twins exchanged made it seem otherwise. Ree felt her face begin to heat.

"Well, I guess we should get started," she said hastily.

Half an hour later, every last paper from the stack had been signed or initialed and the deed was done. Or, more accurately, the deed had exchanged hands.

They had agreed that Saybrook's would take immediate possession of the structure, and so all the utilities and telephone service would be transferred to the resort's account by the end of the business day. Ree now had it in writing that she would reside on the Peril Pointe property, overseeing the renovation as an independent contractor and receiving free board for the duration of her employment.

She stared at the cashier's check in her hands and counted the zeroes. She couldn't believe the sum she would soon deposit into her bank account—the same account that a mere hour ago had been in serious jeopardy of being overdrawn. She wouldn't have to worry about that now or for the foreseeable future if she lived frugally and invested wisely.

For the first time since returning to northern Michigan, she felt herself breathe easier. She might no longer own the Victorian or the waterfront acreage she'd tramped over as a child, but her future was hardly as gloomy as it had appeared a couple years ago when her marriage had been failing right along with Nonna's health.

"Ree?" Dane spoke her name quietly.

She glanced up to find the others were standing. The meeting was over.

"Sorry." She got to her feet as well.

Hands were shaken, polite words exchanged. Throughout it all, Ree's ears buzzed and her throat ached as emotions tumbled hard and fast, one on top of the other. She tried to process them: relief, gratitude and some guilt, excitement, an odd sense of anticipation and a more understandable sadness. And she knew, if she didn't get out of there quickly, she would do something foolish and embarrassing like cry or laugh—perhaps both at the same time.

Even so, after she pulled on her coat and headed toward the exit, she hesitated in the doorway. The lawyers were gone, so it was just Luke, Ali and Audra now. And Dane, of course. Dane, whose kiss had once made Ree forget everything but what it was to feel alive and desired.

Turning back to face them, she said, "I want to thank you, again, for buying Peril Pointe. I know it's in good hands. My grandmother would be pleased. I wish she could have met you all. She would respect the way you do business, putting quality above the bottom line. And she would like you personally because you're good people, good-hearted."

"That's a lovely thing to say," Ali replied.

"Yes, thank you," Luke murmured. He'd been raised by his grandmother as well, Ree recalled from a magazine article. She saw understanding in his kind expression.

"I hope it helps to know you'll be part of the renovations," Audra said. "Part of restoring the house to its original glory."

Ree smiled now. "It does. And I want to thank you for that opportunity as well. Dane told me that you and Ali suggested it."

"We did?" Audra said at the same time Ali piped up with, "He said what?"

Dane cleared his throat noisily, a damning flush staining his cheeks.

"It's really not important who actually decided Ree was a good choice for the job. What's important now is that we've entered into what hopefully will prove to be a profitable venture for Saybrook's."

"Uh-huh." Audra crossed her arms over her chest.

Ali struck a similar pose. "Whatever you say."

Luke kept his mouth firmly closed. Even so Ree

couldn't help noticing how hard he was working to suppress a grin.

After a muttered curse, Dane announced, "I need to make a phone call."

Ree watched him go, a mixture of elation and nerves assailing her. The fact that the job offer had been entirely Dane's doing, touched her deeply. And because it did, it left her feeling vulnerable.

There was nothing between the two of them but the contract they'd just signed. Dane had made it clear that his interest in her was purely business. When Ree was using her head, she knew that was for the best. The problem was, more and more often when it came to Dane Conlan, she found herself leading with her heart.

CHAPTER SEVEN

REE intended to go directly home, where she planned to put on some comfortable clothes, crank up her Three Tenors CD on the stereo and spend the rest of the afternoon in the kitchen making rigatoni from scratch using Nonna's recipe. Maybe she'd stop at the little wine shop near the dock on her way home and pick up a bottle of Chianti so that she could alternately wallow in self-pity and celebrate her life's new direction.

In the parking lot, however, she discovered to her embarrassment that her car wouldn't start. She listened to the finicky engine whine and whir during half a dozen attempts before finally giving up. She was going to have to call a tow truck and she hoped to God that whatever was wrong with the Beetle could be fixed at an island repair shop in relatively short order.

As she withdrew the key from the ignition, someone tapped on the window. She turned to find Dane hunched over.

"Car trouble again?" he asked once she'd manually cranked down the glass.

"Yes. Oliver's being temperamental."

"Oliver."

Dane rested his elbows on the open window frame and shook his head slowly. Amusement brimmed in his eyes.

The rain had subsided into a fine mist, leaving droplets of water sprinkled in his dark hair. Without thinking, Ree reached up and ran the tips of her fingers through the short layers at his temple. Afterward, they simply stared at one another.

"You're getting wet," Ree said at last, hoping her words served as enough of an explanation for the intimate way in which she had just touched him.

Dane didn't say anything, but after a long moment, he reached through the window. She felt a featherlight touch on her cheek, as if his fingertips had just barely grazed its slope on the way to tuck a handful of hair behind her ear.

Then he straightened and the connection she'd felt— the connection that had gone well beyond the mere physical—was broken once again.

"You're dry…but stranded." He smiled, his tone matter-of-fact, and Ree wondered if she had merely imagined the interest that had sparked in his eyes.

"You really need to trade in this heap. I think it's safe to say you can afford more reliable, not to mention stylish, transportation now." He thumped the roof of her car with one hand.

"Trade in Oliver? Are you crazy? A new…*engine* and he'll be running like a dream."

Dane rolled his eyes. Reaching inside his suit coat, he retrieved the cell phone clipped to his belt. "Your best bet for fast turnaround service is The Island Garage. Dial information for the telephone number and have them connect you."

As Ree spoke to the mechanic, Dane let himself in the passenger side, apparently deciding not to stand out in the rain any longer. Ree had brought a photo album she'd found while cleaning out the attic earlier in the week. The cover was faded and the binding frayed, but it was stuffed with priceless pictures of the house.

She had intended to leave it with the Conlans, but then she'd forgotten it in the car before their meeting. Dane had to move it take his seat. Now, as she finished her call, he opened it.

"Well?" he asked when she hung up and handed back the phone.

"Someone named Lester assured me that a tow truck will be out to pick up my Beetle within the hour. He said they have a loaner I can use until they figure out what the problem is. Do you know the time?"

Dane glanced at his watch. "It's nearly noon." After a moment's hesitation, he said, "I was just on my way to have lunch. Why don't you come with me?" Tapping the cover of the photo album with his index finger, he added, "We can go through these pictures and I can tell you a little about the contractors we're considering for the job."

Dane sat next to Ree in a booth at the back of The Sand-piper and tried to concentrate on the photos. It was damned hard when he kept catching faint whiffs of her perfume and stray curls from her hair teased his cheek whenever he leaned in to inspect the pictures. The woman had seriously gorgeous hair. He'd been surprised that she'd left it down today.

The last time she'd worn her sexy little black suit, she'd pulled back her hair in some clip or another. Angry as Dane had been with her at the time, his fingers had itched to set it free. Earlier, at her car, he'd given in to the urge to touch her, touch her hair. He was paying for that now. He knew he would continue to pay late into the night.

"As you can see, the photos are a little out of order," she said, pointing to a Polaroid that had been affixed to one of the pages.

Dane dragged his mind out of the pool of hormones it had been happily drowning in and looked at the picture she was indicating. In it, Ree stood on the porch dressed in a full-length gown. Standing next to her was a gangly limbed boy decked out in an ill-fitting tuxedo.

"Prom?" he asked.

"Sadie-Hawkins Dance my freshman year of high school."

"Nice 'do."

"It was the nineties," she replied defensively. "Big hair was still in." But after studying it another moment, she admitted, "Okay, I'll regret that hairstyle until the day I die. The only comfort is knowing that just about every girl in my high school wore hers the same way."

"Who's the guy?"

"Joshua Borders. He played saxophone in the high school's jazz band. He was a junior," she confided.

"An older man," Dane mused.

"I had a major crush on him, but my grandparents wouldn't let me date yet because I was only fifteen. They made an exception for the dance, but only on the condition that my grandfather drove us."

Dane winced on her behalf. "Ooh…embarrassing."

"Tell me about it. My grandparents were a little… overzealous in some regards," Ree said. "I think they worried I'd turn out like my mother."

"Like your mother?"

She fiddled with the album's frayed binding for a moment before admitting, "She wound up pregnant at eighteen."

"That's awfully young for so much responsibility. You mentioned that your father wasn't around much while you were growing up."

"Actually he wasn't around at all." She looked up then, her gaze open, her tone confidential. "He was married. Still is as far as I know. My mother was an extramarital affair and I was…a mistake."

Dane said nothing, not sure what words were appropriate given the obvious pain the topic caused her.

Ree apparently interpreted his silence differently. "You're probably thinking the apple doesn't fall far from the tree when it comes to honoring wedding vows—"

"No, I wasn't," he interrupted. He couldn't have her believing that. It was better—certainly smarter—to keep all their current dealings impersonal and professional, but he would have to be inhuman not to be affected by such revelations.

So much heartache, so much loss, and Regina had absorbed it all.

"You're not a mistake, Ree. Not then. Not now."

Silence stretched between them. His words, Dane realized, could be taken another way. Lost in her dark eyes, he wasn't sure exactly how he'd meant them.

Finally Ree tucked the photograph carefully back into the plastic sleeve. When she turned the page and launched into a monologue on the background of one of the ensuing photographs, he knew the subject had been dropped.

That was for the best. Wasn't it?

"I don't recall seeing a rose trellis off the side of the front porch," Dane said. "Is it still there?"

"No." Ree grimaced. "My grandmother had a real green thumb, but once she became ill she wasn't able to take care of her flower beds. By the time I moved back, several of the rosebushes, including the climbers, had been seriously damaged by insects and disease. I cut them back, hoping for the best. But only one of them made it through the winter and it didn't flower this year."

"I hear roses can be difficult and a lot of work. Maybe we should go with something that requires a little less care."

"Oh, no. They're worth the work."

She said something else, a couple Italian words whose silky syllables set off an atomic blast in his libido.

"Wh-what was that?"

"Just something my grandmother used to say. Something about how rose petals are tiny treasures sent from heaven."

"Saybrook's has a grounds crew that sees to the

resort's landscaping and maintenance. I'll send some workers over when the time comes. You can tell them about the roses and offer suggestions if you'd like."

She smiled fully and his heart seemed to buck against his ribs. "Thanks, Dane. I have lots of ideas."

She turned the page. "Ooh, here's a good one of the house. This one was taken before my grandparents owned it, back when they used to come to the Petoskey area to vacation."

Dane leaned over for a closer look and his heart thumped again when Ree scooped the hair back from one side of her face, securing it on the other side of her neck with one hand. The move was practical given the way it kept tickling his cheek. But it left her neck exposed and all but begging to be nuzzled.

He gave himself points for self-control when he not only ignored the impulse but managed to sound completely normal.

"Too bad it's black and white. I'm curious about the colors that were used originally on the home's exterior."

"Why?"

She sat back, let her hair loose. It tumbled around her shoulder and his mind went blank.

"Why what?

"Why are you curious about the exterior colors?" Ree said on a laugh.

He cleared his throat and glanced back at the photograph, trying to recall his last coherent thought.

"I, um, I guess I would like the restoration to be as authentic as possible once it's complete. We tried to do that with the resort and so far the feedback from guests

has been very favorable. People have a strong attachment to the past."

"That's not always healthy," Ree noted and Dane
wondered if she truly understood that.

"No, but in this case, it's good for business."

But Ree was shaking her head. "I don't know. I'm
not so sure we'll want to replicate the original paint job.
I've been doing a little more research on Queen Anne-
style Victorians. The color schemes were varied, with
individual homes decked out in a virtual rainbow of
hues. But overall the color palette tended to be dark."

"How dark?"

"Think sienna reds, browns and burnt yellows."

"Hmm, not quite what I'm picturing for Saybrook's
on the Pointe," Dane admitted.

"Me, either. Not with Lake Michigan and those small
dunes as the backdrop. Too romantic."

And Dane recalled that they had been—for a while,
at least, while he'd gazed out at them from her kitchen
window the morning after the big storm.

"So you think we should keep it white?" he asked.

"No. A lot of the ones in town have gone to pastels
and I don't see anything wrong with that." Pointing to
the picture again, she tapped various parts of the house.
"I'm thinking lighter shades of blue, lavender and
mauve or maybe even pink."

She smiled at him, obviously pleased. Dane could
envision the house she described right down to the roof
finials, crestings and gingerbread trim. But he knew
that wasn't what he was referring to when he said,
"You've got me intrigued."

* * *

Ree was cocooning her grandmother's china in bubble wrap when Audra telephoned Ree late the following day with a surprising invitation.

"My husband has a show in the new gallery on Trillium this weekend and we were wondering if you would like to attend? Seth would love to meet you."

"I didn't realize you were married to an artist," Ree said, shifting the cordless phone to her other shoulder and reaching for another dinner plate.

"Seth's not an artist in that sense of the word. He's a photographer. Nature now, human nature before," Audra added on a laugh. "That's actually how we met."

"I see."

Audra's laughter trilled again. "No you don't, but I appreciate your politeness. Seth was a tabloid photographer who took some really horrible shots of me back when I was, well, to put it mildly, a self-destructive idiot. He had his reasons for doing what he did, reasons that aren't important now. What is important is that he saved my life…in more ways than one."

"I'd say you're both very lucky then."

"Yes." Audra sighed, and then sniffled. "Sorry. Damned hormones. Anyway, I know the invitation is very last minute, but we were thinking that if you were free, maybe you could join us Saturday night."

Ree absently snapped a few of the wrap's air-filled pockets.

"Will, um, Ali be there?" she asked, even though that wasn't the Conlan sibling whose whereabouts really interested her.

"Yes and Luke." After a short pause, Audra added, "Dane, too, of course. He wouldn't miss it."

"It sounds like a real family affair."

"Oh, you wouldn't be intruding. There will be lots of other guests, half of whom I will hardly know. Besides, this will give you a chance to meet my husband and get to know all of us a little better now that you're working with us."

Ree couldn't have said why, but she felt there was more than that behind the invitation. Even so, she accepted. What else did she have to do on a Saturday night?

"What do you mean, Regina Bellini will be there?" Dane said.

It was Friday evening and Seth, Audra and he had just finished dinner. Dane was a frequent guest at their table. On this night Audra had invited him over for grilled pork chops in a mango-basil sauce she'd prepared herself. Throughout her pregnancy she'd had cravings—not for bizarre concoctions, but for five-star restaurant-quality food. Sometimes she had the entire meal flown in, sometimes just all the fresh ingredients. All Dane could say was God bless impending motherhood, especially since he didn't have to live with her and bear the brunt of her wild mood swings.

The food was delicious as usual, but his sister's bombshell as she served dessert had all that perfectly grilled pork turning to a lead weight in the pit of his stomach. He eyed the slice of cherry upside down cake Audra had set on the table in front of him. No way he was going to be able to enjoy it now. What a waste.

"I invited her to Seth's show, that's what I mean," Audra repeated as if she were talking to a slow child.

"Why? You barely know her."

"I know her enough to like her. Besides, she's working for Saybrook's now. I invited some of the other people we have on our payroll."

"Well you might have cleared it with me first," Dane grumbled.

It wasn't that he didn't want to see Ree again. He did. A little *too* much, which was why he'd been planning to let a good week pass before they started the restoration work that would put them in close proximity on a regular basis for the next several months.

Audra's eyes narrowed. It was her turn to ask, "Why? I thought whatever misunderstanding you two had had was old news. Do you still have a problem with Regina?"

"No." Other than the fact that being around her was pure torture. For the first time in his life, Dane thought he understood perfectly why moths fluttered around lightbulbs, getting so close they sometimes wound up being incinerated. That's how he felt whenever he was near Ree. Desperate. Doomed.

"Then what's the big deal?"

Dane glanced at Seth for support, but his brother-in-law pushed back from the table. "Oh, no. Don't try to drag me into this. Think of me as Switzerland: neutral."

"Neutral. I've got another word for it," Dane muttered. "Doesn't it bother you that your wife is like a pit bull."

"It's a Conlan family trait," Seth mused as he left the room. "One head is harder than the next."

Audra let their comments slide. "I don't need your

permission to be friendly, Dane. I like Ree. I thought she would enjoy Seth's show and having a night out. She's in that big house all by herself while her husband is away."

"He's not just *away.*"

Dane knew he'd made a fatal error when he spied the gleam in his sister's eye. "Oh?"

Grudgingly he admitted, "They're legally separated, okay."

"I knew it! I *knew* something was going on. Especially with the way you—" She broke off abruptly.

No doubt he would regret asking, but he did so anyway. "The way I what?"

She forked up a dainty bite of cake and ate it before answering. "You're interested in her, Dane. It's obvious. It's also obvious that the attraction is not all one-sided. Something is going on between you two."

"Aud." He grabbed his sister's left hand and tapped meaningfully on her diamond ring with the tip of his index finger. "She's a *married* woman. There's *nothing* going on between us."

"You just said she was separated."

Dane cursed in frustration, not so much at Audra's meddling as at the damnable situation. "That's a divorce decree away from being single."

"Try not to judge her too harshly," Audra said, her expression sobering.

"I'm not." Was he?

His sister waved off his denial. "I've been in that situation. Ending a marriage is painful and unpleasant even when the reasons for being in it have long since run out. Divorce represents failure, Dane. No one likes to fail. Believe me, I know, having done it more times than I care to remember."

He needed to change the subject, so he reached over and gave her bulging belly a pat. "You're happy now, kiddo. That's what counts."

"More than happy," Audra agreed. "And I want that for you, too."

When she walked him to his Trailblazer later that evening, she left him with another piece of advice.

"I meant what I said earlier about not judging Regina too harshly."

"Aud—"

She placed a finger over his mouth. "Let me finish, please. Don't judge yourself too harshly, either."

"I don't know what you mean," he said.

Audra's smile was all-knowing. "You can't help whom you fall for, Dane. Or when. Just look at Seth and me."

Now, as Dane stood in Loraine's Art Gallery only half listening to the chatter of some acquaintances he knew through Saybrook's, he mulled Audra's words. His sister was probably right about the painfulness of Ree's situation. No one liked to fail. For Ree it had to be especially difficult. Reading between the lines it was clear that her parents' marital status had put pressure on her to make her own marriage work. Also clear was the fact that she loved her grandparents dearly and had wanted their approval. Even now, though both of them were gone, she tried to honor their memory.

When Ree arrived half an hour later, the gallery was even more packed with what seemed like half the population of the island sampling hors d'oeuvres, drinking champagne and admiring Seth's handiwork. Despite the milling crowd, Dane spotted her right away. She was a hard woman to miss even wearing an understated black pullover and a pair of wide-legged tan trousers.

It was that hair, he decided, and let out slowly the air that had backed up in his lungs.

She was glancing around, looking uncomfortable, when he walked over carrying two flutes of champagne.

He handed her one. "Have you had a chance to meet Seth yet?" he asked.

Dane knew perfectly well that she hadn't, but he didn't want her to know that he'd spent the past half hour eyeing the door and waiting for her to walk through it.

"Hello, Dane. No, I haven't met him. I only just arrived a moment ago." She glanced around again. "I was looking for Audra. I figured once I spotted her I'd be able to figure out the identity of the guest of honor."

"Why don't you let me take the guesswork out of it for you?"

Within short order the introduction was accomplished. In addition to meeting Seth, Ree chatted easily with Dane's sisters and greeted Luke as well. She fit in well with them, he couldn't help but notice, and they made her feel welcome.

As more people came up to congratulate Audra's husband on his artistry with a camera, Dane suggested to Ree that they walk through the exhibit.

The gallery was small, but its space was put to good use. Seth's photographs had been framed and matted. Some were grouped by subject matter—trees, flowers, animals, insects. Others hung alone for a more potent effect. Most were in full color, but there were a few striking black-and-whites.

"He's very talented," Ree said. "He has a real knack for capturing a single moment in nature."

They were standing before a photograph of a large black and yellow spider. Its dewy orb-shaped web was suspended between the twin trunks of a white birch tree and glinted seductively in the morning sun.

"It's funny how the things we should avoid can sometimes be so…irresistible," Dane murmured. A waiter walked by and Dane snagged two fresh flutes of champagne from the tray. He held one out to Ree.

She took it and sipped, the fizzy wine giving her the courage to say, "Isn't it?"

A look passed between them and she thought Dane would say something more. He didn't, though, moving on to the next photograph instead. They circled the room without speaking again, not that words were necessary when every glance seemed to hold meaning.

They ended up near the door, which someone had cracked open. It relieved Ree to know she wasn't the only person who'd grown intolerably warm.

"The air feels good," she said and laughed nervously as she fanned her heated face.

Dane had removed his sports coat and loosened his tie earlier, but he didn't look any cooler than she. In fact, he pulled the tie free now and stuffed it into the back pocket of his trousers before undoing another button on his shirt.

"Want to step outside?" he asked.

She should say no, but what came out was, "Maybe just for a moment."

They walked down the street, past a row of quaint little gift shops that had long since closed, some for the day and some for the season. But the little Irish pub on the corner was open and doing a brisk business judging from the number of cars turning into its lot and the raucous laughter spilling from its open doors.

"Want to get a drink?" Dane asked.

"Better not. I think that champagne went to my head," Ree confessed. "I ate a light dinner."

"We could grab a bite?"

Because that sounded entirely too wonderful, she said, "Nah, I'm not really that hungry. Maybe we could just walk a little more."

The waterfront was a block ahead. Dane steered her in that direction. Just to the north of where the ferries berthed, a wooden walkway flanked the water's edge, winding all the way to a state park's public beach and picnic area. Benches were sprinkled along it, as were lights. It seemed to Ree that she and Dane had the island to themselves as they walked, cocooned in twilight and serenaded by the gentle swell and break of the waves.

When they stopped at one of the benches, Dane offered her his jacket, which she gratefully accepted. She was no longer warm. The air held the bite of fall and the breeze had picked up, carrying the scents of cedar and woodsmoke from the fire pit outside a nearby weekender's cottage.

From their vantage point they could see the lights of Petoskey as well as the lights of the car ferry making its run from the mainland.

"The last scheduled ferry leaves at eleven," he said conversationally. "Summer hours ended with Labor Day."

"I'd better make sure I'm on it. That's a long swim and I'm not particularly fond of the water," she joked.

Dane was serious when he asked, "Does it bother you, living by the water, when your mother drowned?" He retracted the question instantly. "I'm sorry, Ree. That's probably not something you want to talk about."

"Actually I never *have* talked about it," she admitted, just having realized that was true. "My grandparents were so devastated by my mother's death, they didn't speak of it. Other than putting up the memorial, they never referred to it again. At least not in front of me."

"That's understandable. They say there's nothing worse than losing a child."

"Especially to suicide," she murmured, not even aware she'd said the words aloud until Dane replied, "God, Ree, I had no idea."

"It's okay. How would you? It's not something I mention often. In fact, I've never told anyone."

"Not even your husband?" he asked quietly.

"No. Not even Paul."

She had laid a reassuring hand on his arm as she spoke. When she drew it away now, he reached for it, held on. The simple contact gave her strength to remember, to reexamine.

"I used to wonder if I was the reason she walked into the lake."

"No." He squeezed her fingers for emphasis. "I'm sure you weren't. People who take their lives are depressed, confused. You can't blame yourself, especially when you were just a kid."

Ree nodded. She believed that…most of the time. But sometimes doubts still niggled. She listened to the waves now. They were much calmer than they had been that day so long ago.

"You want to talk about it?" Dane asked.

She didn't, no. What would be the point? Yet, she heard herself say, "I remember that she smiled at me. She was already in the water, walking out, and she turned at the waist and smiled. 'Stay on the shore,' she told me. Then she was swimming away. I watched and I watched until I couldn't see her anymore. Then I waited. I waited in that spot just up the dune every night, hoping that somehow she would come back."

"The gazebo," Dane said.

Even on the dimly lit boardwalk she knew her surprise had to be obvious. "How did you guess?"

"You said your grandparents built it when you were just a girl. And that day we came to see the property you mentioned that you liked to play there, pretending you were the keeper of a lighthouse beacon."

"I wanted her to be able to see our home and swim toward it," Ree admitted. "It was…silly."

"Not so silly. I saw your light. I swam toward it. I was saved."

She was silent for a moment, but then she faced him. "What about you? Does the water bother you now?"

"I thought it would, but no. I credit you for that." He brushed his knuckles across her cheek. God, she needed him to touch her. "That was the most unforgettable night of my life…and not because ᶠ my accident or the storm."

When he kissed her, it was like celebrating a homecoming. It felt so right.

"I still want you, Ree."

Her heart skipped a beat at the words, but then he pulled back. Back, but not away. He remained so close that Ree could feel his breath, ragged and hot, as it disturbed her hair, but he didn't kiss her again. His mouth hovered mere inches from her face and so she took matters into her own hands, closing the last bit of space so she could settle her lips over his.

She heard him groan, felt his fingers snake into her hair, fist there. Need had simmered for so long that it boiled over now, engulfing them both.

"Please," she whispered, begging for what exactly she wasn't sure.

He angled his head, deepened the kiss.

"I know," he murmured against her lips.

They had been here before. Exactly here, except that instead of being pressed up against the unforgiving edge of her kitchen cupboards, it was the wooden slats of a public bench that bit into her spine now. She didn't care.

But then the ferry's horn blasted rudely as the boat neared the dock several dozen yards down the shoreline. Ree and Dane shot apart guiltily.

Ree said nothing. Dane was not silent. Cursing, he got to his feet and paced several yards away.

"I don't know what I'm thinking. We can't do this. It's wrong. A mistake."

"Don't call it that," she begged hoarsely. The old hurt warring with this new one. "Not a mistake."

Dane sighed heavily. "I'm sorry."

He hadn't meant to wound her with that ill-chosen word, but he couldn't think straight. All he knew was that if he didn't have her, he'd go insane. Yet, if he crossed that line, breached his own moral code, he wouldn't be able to live with himself.

"I'm trying to do the right thing here, Ree."

"I think you just did."

When Regina stood and reached out to him, he backed farther away. He had to keep his distance.

"No. It's not right. You're married."

"Paul and I are sep—"

"You're married," he finished for her. He scrubbed a hand over his face. "I think we both need to re-member that."

CHAPTER EIGHT

BY THE end of October, Dane and Ree had settled into a fairly predictable work routine. On Mondays, they touched base mainly by telephone if something had come up over the weekend. Otherwise, Ree used the time for research and Dane went about his business at the resort.

He had insisted on setting her up with a laptop computer, Internet access, a cell phone and a personal digital assistant, telling her they were necessary tools for her work with Saybrook's. She had pointed out that as an independent contractor, it should be up to her to supply such items. He overruled her arguments, though, and she finally gave up. Dane Conlan, she realized, could be incredibly pigheaded.

On Fridays, Ree took the ferry over to the island to meet with Dane, his sisters and Luke and bring them up to speed on the project. It only took an hour, more or less, and Dane had suggested they could easily do it by conference call since he knew Ree wasn't fond of the water, but she'd been the pigheaded one on that issue.

She preferred seeing them all face-to-face. Besides, it got her out of the house. With the weather turning colder and the days growing shorter, she'd begun to feel too isolated. And, with the first anniversary of her grandmother's death approaching, she also felt even more alone. So, on Fridays she headed to the resort.

It was the other three days of the week, though, that Ree really looked forward to. On Mondays, Tuesdays and Wednesdays, Dane came over to the mainland and they pored over plans. He arrived at her home by nine, usually bearing bagels or the occasional calorie-laden pastry he'd picked up at the bakery on Trillium. Ree supplied the coffee and they sat in her kitchen, heads together, various notes and blueprints spread over the table.

They rarely strayed to personal topics. He didn't bring up her marital status again and so she didn't inform him when she called her lawyer to move ahead with divorce proceedings in spite of her absentee husband's lack of consent. It would take a couple of months at least to obtain a default judgment. In the meantime, Ree decided it was for the best that she and Dane had returned to more neutral footing.

What bothered her, though, was how easily he'd managed that transition. He appeared completely immune to the simmering sexual tension that had Ree wanting to crack the windows and let in the crisp autumn air.

Immune except for when, at the start of that first meeting one week after the fiasco on the boardwalk, he'd made an unusual request. As they'd glanced through some photographs Dane had pulled from the

Internet, she'd gathered up her hair and pulled it to the side so she could lean closer. The weather was damp though, and her hair a rioting mess. Finally she'd plucked up the rubber band that had been wound around a sheaf of blueprints and used it to secure her ponytail.

A moment later, Ree had held her breath while Dane gently removed it.

"Leave your hair down," he'd said. Nothing more.

He'd given her no reason for his preference and Ree had been too startled, too damned turned on by the smoldering look in his eyes, to ask for one. Since then, even though she sometimes itched to pull it back and out of the way, she never did on the days he came.

They had hired a contractor whose specialty was renovating historic properties. His name was Case Portman and he was well-regarded for his accuracy and attention to detail. He'd honed his skills in southern cities, notably restoring some of Charleston's most storied homes, before moving to the Midwest. His wife hailed from the region and her ill health had prompted their return so she could be closer to family.

These days, he had plenty of work refurbishing the grand ladies found along Lake Michigan's shore. From her research, Ree knew that before the turn of the twentieth century, the huge homes had been built by industrialists and other affluent families, who'd used them to escape the heat and congestion of the city in the summer. Now, many of them had been changed into bed-and-breakfasts.

Case was finishing up another project nearby in

Petoskey and wouldn't be coming on board for another month. Even so, work had already begun on the home's exterior. Dane had determined that the roof repairs couldn't wait and so Ree's first official task had been to select new fish-scale shingles to replace the existing ones.

Some mornings, when Case had an hour or two of downtime from his other obligations, he dropped in while Dane was at Peril Pointe. More often than not, though, it was just Ree and Dane in the sprawling and now sparsely furnished Victorian.

With the exception of Ree's bedroom suite and the kitchen table, her grandmother's other furnishings, including area rugs and wall hangings, had been moved to storage. It made sense, of course, since new furniture and accessories would be purchased for the bed-and-breakfast. Dane was leaving that task to Ree as well. Even so, the big house seemed much less cheery now that it had so little to absorb the echoes from her footsteps as she paced the hardwood floors.

She supposed that was why she looked forward to Dane's thrice-weekly arrival. Each time the bell chimed, a kick of adrenaline revved through her system. And when he pushed back from the table, the scrape of chair legs signaling the conclusion of their discussion, she felt the first prick of loneliness.

He was gone by noon, and though she supposed it was foolish, Ree always saw him out, walking with him to the front door and then standing in the big bay window. Her grandmother's hand-tatted lace curtains were gone, leaving nothing to obstruct Ree's view as she watched the Trailblazer idle down the long driveway and pull out onto the main road. Afterward, she returned to the kitchen and occupied her time going over architectural research or on the telephone to various suppliers trying to track down vintage fixtures.

That was her plan on this day, but as she watched, the Trailblazer stopped halfway down the driveway, shifted into Reverse and sped back to the house.

Ree walked onto the porch and, as Dane got out of his vehicle, she called, "Forget something?"

"Sort of." He jiggled the keys in his hand. "I was wondering if you might have a suggestion for a gift for Audra and Seth's baby. She'll be born any day now and I still haven't gotten anything. Ali suggested a keepsake locket or other jewelry since the kid already has just about everything else. But I don't know."

"There's a little shop in town that has some really adorable, one-of-a-kind outfits. They're handmade and come with matching shoes."

Dane's expression brightened. "Shoes. Aud is big into shoes. She has a special walk-in closet in her new home dedicated to footwear. *Her* footwear. I don't think she allows Seth's best loafers to share shelf space."

"There you go, then," Ree said on a grin. "The perfect gift."

He nodded, jiggled the keys some more. Cocking his head to one side, he said, "So, want to play hooky for the rest of the day and come with me?"

The invitation surprised Ree as much as it delighted her, but she managed to keep her tone casual. "Does this mean my boss is giving me permission to cut work and shop for shoes?"

"Shoes for a *baby*," he replied with mock sternness. "And don't think you're going to drag me into every shop and boutique in Petoskey. We'll hit the one you mentioned, I'll buy something for the baby and that will be the end of it."

"Little girls grow up to be women," she reminded him.

He muttered what sounded like, "Yes, and God help the other half of the population," although she was too far away to be sure.

"Stick with me and I could have you set for the next eighteen or so birthdays."

He waved in the direction of the front door. "Go get your coat and whatever else you need before I change my mind about springing you for the day."

Dane never would have guessed that shopping could be an almost erotic experience. But it was with Ree. She was passionate about everything—oohing and ahhing over crocheted booties, closing her eyes dreamily as she rubbed a monogrammed satin comforter against her cheek, clutching at his arm in excitement when she spied a hand-carved and hand-painted rocking horse.

He told himself he found it annoying and that was why he gritted his teeth each time one of those appreciative little noises hummed from her throat. But he knew he was a liar. The truth was, even knowing he couldn't have Ree hadn't stopped him from wanting her.

Once upon a time, he'd foolishly hoped their forced proximity would file the dangerous edge off his attraction, but he'd been sadly mistaken. The more time he spent with Ree, the more he liked her and the more he wanted to be with her. Of course, his hormones had been engaged since she'd flung open the door of her Victorian that first night. Now, it went much deeper than that. He appreciated her dry sense of humor, her innate curiosity, her work ethic, her sheer will. She'd handled so much heartache and she'd done so with grace and courage and an abiding love for the grandparents who had stepped into the breech and raised a young girl.

Recalling his conversation with Ree on that long-ago stormy night, he decided they would be proud of the way she had thrown herself into the renovation project, making lemonade from the lemons life had handed her. Hell, *he* was proud of her.

"Why are you looking at me like that?" she asked and Dane realized he'd been caught staring.

"Just, uh, wondering if coming here before eating lunch was such a smart idea. I'm probably going to starve to death before you make up your mind," he evaded smoothly.

She made a face at him and went back to inspecting the store's goods. They had spent the past forty-five minutes in the same specialty boutique—and they still hadn't made it to the display of hand-sewn baby outfits and shoes Ree had mentioned. She said she just wanted to *look*, since she, too, planned to purchase something for Audra's baby. Every time Dane thought Ree had finally made her selection, though, she changed her mind.

For the past several minutes she'd had her eye on a miniature tea service. She'd even peppered the saleswoman with questions about how easily replacement pieces could be found since it was made of fine bone china and something was bound to get broken over the years.

"So, are you going to buy it?" Dane asked when the saleswoman had gone to help another customer.

"I think so." Ree glanced past him then and her eyes grew round. "Oh my God!"

On the table in the middle of the store was a scaled down version of a Queen Anne-style Victorian that was eerily reminiscent of her Peril Pointe home.

She rushed over, making those sexy little noises all the way, and then bent to peek through the windows of the fully furnished dollhouse. The pose and her nicely rounded posterior did things for a couple plain denim pockets that Dane decided should be illegal.

"You've got to check this out," she said.

Gaze still riveted to her bottom, Dane murmured, "Oh, I am. Believe me, I am."

But then he walked over and peered inside, unable to resist the awe and excitement brimming in her tone.

"I always wanted one of these when I was a girl," she mused after a dreamy sigh. "My grandfather tried to make me one for my tenth birthday. It was a kit and he had it nearly assembled and ready for painting. He'd hidden it in the attic so I wouldn't find it. He wanted it to be a surprise."

Dane turned so he could see her face. She looked so beautiful, caught up in memories, these ones apparently good. "What happened?"

"The surprise turned out to be that our roof had a leak and the dollhouse was ruined before I ever got to play with it." She shook her head, and though she had to have been disappointed at the time, she was grinning now. "I was already pretty fluent in Italian, but I became bilingual in cursing that day."

"Your nonna couldn't have been pleased."

"No." She chuckled.

They both straightened.

"I think I'll go with the tea service," she said.

"Not the dollhouse?"

"It's kind of an extravagant gift for a, um, work acquaintance," she replied, and he got the feeling the bland description was for his benefit, since he knew Ree, Ali and Audra had lunch every Friday after their meeting at Saybrook's. And the other night, his sisters had met Ree in Petoskey to go to the movies. "Even the tea service is a bit over the top, but I can afford it now. Besides, I really like Audra. And Ali, too."

That should bother him, Dane thought. Or, at the very least, he should be indifferent to the fact his sisters and Ree enjoyed one another's company and had common interests that transcended work. Yet he found their burgeoning friendship damned pleasing, and he tried not to recall that, while always polite, Ali and Audra had never really warmed up to Julie to the point where the women hung out together.

Forty minutes later, he and Ree were seated inside a small bistro that faced the water. The waitress had taken their orders and brought their beverages. Ree had her fingers wrapped around her coffee cup for warmth. They'd stowed their packages in his car, which they left parked near the boutique. Ree had talked him into walking to the eatery on the pretext that it was good exercise. He now suspected it had more to do with the fact she'd wanted to window-shop along the way than any desire to improve her cardiovascular health.

"Audra is going to die when she opens your gift," she told him. "The embroidery on that pinafore is a work of art. And those little shoes…" A smile curved her lips and she hummed.

Dane burned.

"What is it about women and shoes?" he asked, forcing his thoughts well below her knees and even then his mind came up with fantasies.

Ree raised an eyebrow in challenge. "What is it about men and power tools?"

"Tools are useful. You can build things with them, fix stuff."

"Are you saying shoes aren't useful?"

"Okay, they're *useful*. But how many pairs do you need?"

"Do you have a handsaw?"

"Yeah." He nodded slowly, already wary of the smug superiority he saw in her expression. Audra and Ali often got that look right before they landed a verbal punch he hadn't seen coming.

"A power saw?"

"Sure, but—"

"A chain saw?" she interrupted.

"Two, actually," he admitted. When she merely blinked, he explained, "But only because I needed something with a bit more horsepower to tackle a big oak that fell across my driveway after an ice storm last winter."

"So, you have a lot of different saws, but you *use* them all. You *need* them all."

"Oh, no." He shook his head. "It's not the same."

"It is. Men can get away with the same pair of wingtips with just about every suit they own. Women's wardrobes require variety, especially since one outfit can be paired with different shoes for a totally different effect."

"I'm not even going to ask," he muttered.

"Because you know I'm right." She sighed then, apparently deciding he'd already accepted defeat. "God, I've really missed shopping for shoes."

Pumps and power tools—their conversation was so ridiculous, Dane couldn't help but laugh. Amazingly he was having the best time he'd had in weeks...maybe even longer. It was on the tip of his tongue to tell her that. Thankfully the waitress arrived with their meals, sparing them both the awkwardness such an inappropriate confession would create.

Ree had ordered California chicken salad in a pita pocket. When their meals came, however, she surprised him by picking up her fork and shaving off a sliver from one of the meatballs on his submarine sandwich. After popping it into her mouth and chewing, she made a comical face.

"They call those meatballs," she tsked after glancing over her shoulder to be sure the waitress was out of earshot.

Dane eyed the sub. "What's wrong with them?"

"Nothing. I'm sure they're fine. They're just not... Italian despite the tomato sauce and mozzarella cheese that have been heaped over top of them."

While they'd shopped, Ree's sound effects had

turned Dane on, but that was nothing compared to the geyser of unadulterated lust that shot through him after hearing her pronounce the word mozzarella.

"S-say that again," he whispered, with all the urgency of an addict.

Ree frowned. "Say what again?"

"Mozzarella."

Her brows remained tugged together as she repeated the word, turning four seemingly innocuous syllables into what might as well have been foreplay in his mind.

Dane swallowed hard and closed his eyes on a groan.

"Are you okay?" she asked.

"No." And he meant it. He wasn't all right. He was teetering on a ledge, part of him wanting to jump. Had he ever been this sexually aroused or this sexually frustrated in his adult life?

"I'm sure your sandwich is fine," she assured him, sounding sheepish. "I didn't mean to make you queasy."

God, she thought he was nauseated. Wasn't that a kick in the old ego? Here he was burning up with desire and she believed he was suffering stomach upset.

"I'm not queasy," he said, opening his eyes. "I'm… just forget it." He picked up the sandwich and took a big bite to prove his point.

"How is it?" she asked after a moment.

"Fine." He shrugged. "Tastes Italian to me."

She made a different humming noise then, this one no less unsettling. "Well, that's only because you've never eaten my grandmother's cooking. Her *cannelloni al forno* was the best."

He set the sub back on his plate. She had used that sexy Italian inflection again and he was lost. "Go on. I'm listening."

"Nonna used only the freshest spices and ingredients. And her *pesto con basilico?* Delicious."

She moaned softly and so did he.

"I sometimes ate the pesto without the pasta, spreading it on a thick slice of bread," she was saying.

Lost in those lushly fringed dark eyes, Dane murmured, "Homemade bread, I suppose."

"Homemade bread, homemade pasta. She made it all—linguine, fettuccine, tagliatelle, tortellini." His libido absorbed the hits as she rattled off the varieties.

"Sounds…great," he somehow managed to say.

Ree grinned then and Dane was amazed that he didn't combust given the heat that was singeing his insides. She leaned toward him and in a confidential whisper, admitted, "My grandparents made their own wine, too."

He did his best to corral his stampeding hormones. Food…wine…concentrate, he ordered himself. He thanked his lucky stars that his voice was only marginally hoarse when he asked, "So, where did they get the grapes?"

"On Peril Pointe. Those are grapevines that cover the arbor on the side of house. They don't yield a lot of fruit, but enough for a few bottles of wine. The stuff my grandparents made was pretty good."

Despite Dane's best efforts, his gaze dipped to her lips. "I wouldn't mind sampling some of that," he said.

* * *

Ree wanted the magic of the day to last. The laughter, the teasing…the flirting. This wasn't a date, and yet it was the best one she'd ever been on.

She credited Dane for that. It was so easy to be herself around him. For so long she had been ashamed of her passionate nature. The specter of her mother's ruin had always loomed over Ree's encounters with the opposite sex. Perhaps that's what had made Paul so safe. He'd never been able to make her burn just by staring at her mouth. Nor had he been able to make her laugh so freely…feel so deeply.

In the short span of her association with Dane, Ree had discovered so many things about herself—truths that she'd denied, old wounds that she'd pretended didn't exist. They were healing now. She was healing.

And, for the first time in her life, she was falling in love.

"Ready?" Dane asked, standing to shrug into his coat.

"I am." She meant it.

Soon, soon, she thought, mentally counting off the days on the calendar. If all went well, she would have her divorce not long after the new year.

They returned to the Victorian just after the sun set, having spent another couple hours talking as they browsed through a bookstore and an art gallery before stopping at a small pub just outside town for Irish coffee.

Beneath the laughter and joking, sexual tension simmered and sometimes snapped like an exposed wire. Dane had remained a perfect gentleman, although he had reached across the Trailblazer's console and taken

Ree's hand not long after they settled into their seats. He was still holding it when they reached the house.

The lights were out. Ree hadn't thought to turn any on before leaving earlier in the day. She hadn't expected to return so late. Without so much as a lamp burning, the place looked so cheerless. So lonely.

"Let me walk you to your door," Dane said, letting go of her hand to shift the vehicle into Park and remove the key from the ignition.

"Technically it's your door now." When they were standing before it, she worked up the nerve to ask, "Do you want to come in for a drink or maybe dinner? I have some pesto in the fridge. Nonna's recipe. I made it yesterday."

In the dimness, she couldn't see Dane's expression, but he set down her packages and took the keys from her to unlock. Ree entered, crossing the foyer so she could switch on a light. When she turned, Dane had set her shopping bags just inside the door, but he was still standing on the porch.

"I really should get back." He held out the keys.

"Oh, sure." She nodded, took the keys. "I'm going ahead with the divorce." The words just popped out.

She heard Dane's swift intake of breath and saw his Adam's apple bob in his throat just above the collar of his coat. But he didn't say anything.

"Paul hasn't responded to my previous attempts to end our marriage and I, well, I haven't pushed it. Until now. My lawyer says it will be a little while yet before I can get a default judgment and the divorce is final.

Certain steps have to be taken. But I thought…I thought you should know."

"I don't want to be responsible for that, Ree," he said at last. And she loved Dane all the more for his sense of honor, misplaced though it was.

"You're not. My marriage was over long before I ever met you."

"But you stayed in it."

"It was easier that way." She hadn't had to disappoint her grandmother with a divorce. She hadn't had to admit to herself that she'd made a royal mess of things. The admission was embarrassing but she made it anyway. "I never should have married Paul."

"Did…do you love him?"

"I respected him, admired his intellect. He was a safe choice, but he wasn't the right man. Not for me." She moistened her lips. "I know that now."

"How do you know that?" Dane asked softly.

"You," she said simply.

He still didn't step inside, but the look on his face before he bid Ree good-night told her they had crossed an important threshold.

CHAPTER NINE

THE last Friday in October dawned cold, with frost turning the grounds around the Victorian white. Ree bundled up in a wool coat and drove to the dock, hoping Oliver's sputtering carburetor was not the bad omen that it seemed to be.

On the passenger seat was the gift she'd bought for Audra and Seth's soon-to-be-born baby. She'd wrapped it the night before, after Dane's departure, needing to keep herself occupied. Afterward, she'd cleaned out her closet, putting away the last of her summer things and then sorting the heavier garments to hang by color. Even that tedious chore hadn't kept Ree's mind off the look Dane had given her right before leaving.

Winter was coming, but in her heart, it was spring.

Dane was the only one in the conference room when Ree arrived. He had one hip resting on the low window sill and was just getting ready to take a sip of his coffee. Their gazes locked over the rim and the cup remained a good couple inches from his lips for a long moment before he finally brought it to his mouth and drank deeply.

"Hello, Dane." And because she knew she hadn't, Ree asked, "Sleep well?"

It gratified her immensely when he replied, "No. Tossed and turned all night. You?"

"The same."

"I've been that way a lot lately."

"Me, too."

"They make pills for that, you know." Ali walked in behind Ree. She sent a wink in her brother's direction before grinning at Ree, who felt the color rise in her cheeks.

"Hi, Ali."

"Are you still joining Audra and me for lunch today?" She asked Ree. Glancing toward Dane, she added, "Or have you gotten a better offer?"

"We're still on," Ree confirmed.

Audra walked in then. Or, more accurately, she waddled. Ree couldn't help but grin. "Hi, honey. How are you?"

"How do I look?" Audra grumbled, but then she offered an apologetic smile. "Sorry, I'm just tired of being so huge that I can be spotted from space."

She plopped down on the chair next to Ali, who patted her twin's arm. "You look beautiful, Aud."

"Lovely," Ree seconded.

"Radiant," Dane added hastily after a meaningful look from both Ree and Ali.

Audra didn't appear convinced. "I look like I should be flying over the Rose Bowl, but thanks anyway."

"It won't be much longer," Ree told her.

"No. The doctor said if I haven't gone into labor by

Monday, they're going to induce. And about time, I say." She patted her stomach. "Come on, little one, stop being so stubborn and get out here already."

"Mom says you should try walking or other light activity to get things moving," Ali said. "She said she canned an entire batch of dill pickles just before delivering Dane."

Ree knew from Dane's sisters that their parents had arrived from Florida a week earlier, intent on being in Michigan for the birth of their first grandchild. They were staying with Audra and Seth. Which was why Audra insisted on working. She'd confided to Ree when they went to the movies the other night that her mother's hovering and constant advice were driving her crazy.

"I've worn a path in the carpeting, no luck. Even sex hasn't sent me into labor. And Seth and I have been going at it like bunnies for the past week."

"Aud," Dane murmured, looking uncomfortable.

"What?" She sent him a wicked grin. "Some of us are getting it."

"Getting what?" Luke asked as he walked in.

"Nothing," Dane replied, shooting his sister a black look.

Audra's grin widened. "Exactly."

The meeting got under way then. Since the contractor had been out of town, however, it ended a mere fifteen minutes later.

"Well, that was a short one," Ali said, pushing her chair back from the table.

"I know. Not much new to report since last week, I'm afraid," Ree admitted.

Audra divided a considering look between Regina and Dane. Eyebrows arching, she said, "Hmm, and I got the impression things were progressing."

Dane didn't say anything for a long moment. Then he admitted softly, "They are. Slowly but surely."

His gaze was so steady on Ree that the rest of the room seemed to melt away.

"Yes, slowly but surely," she agreed, working up the audacity to add, "Of course, I'm hoping the pace will pick up soon."

"This kind of thing takes time," Dane countered. "Especially if you want to get it right."

"Oh, I want to get it right."

Luke's discreet cough shattered the moment. "Um, are we still talking about Saybrook's on the Pointe?" he asked.

"I'm not sure," Ali replied. "But I think I might need to take a cold shower."

Ree worried that lunch with Dane's sisters would be awkward after the scene in the conference room. It wasn't, though. Her dealings with his sisters never were.

It amazed Ree how quickly she had come to think of Dane's sisters as friends. She hadn't planned to become chummy with them, any more than she had planned to fall in love with their brother. Technically she was in their employ, at least until the renovation was complete, but they never made Ree feel like anything less than their equal. And she adored them. They were funny, smart, generous and kind to a fault, even as they bickered almost comically over the most mundane things. Sometimes, sitting in their midst, Ree found herself fantasizing about what it would be like to be part of such a family.

They decided to eat in the resort's dining room since Audra had a craving for beef tips and twice-baked potatoes. Almost as soon as they sat down at the table, the bickering began. On this day the topic was nursery colors.

"I think you should have kept the baby's room neutral. That way she will not be subjected to society's stereotypes from the first moment she peeks her head out of the womb," Ali said matter-of-factly as she shook out her napkin and spread it over her lap.

"My daughter's self-esteem will not be in jeopardy just because I've chosen to decorate her room in pink," Audra replied. "Besides, I plan to make sure she knows she can be anything she chooses to be and I expect you, as her godmother, to do your part, too."

"Her godmother," Ali repeated on a sigh that morphed its way into a sob.

"Are you all right?" Ree blinked, stunned and a little panicked. Ali wasn't the overly emotional sort.

Ali waved her hand and then picked up the napkin to dab at her eyes. "Sorry. I'm fine. Really. Just…" She sobbed again. "Just a little teary-eyed today for some reason."

Audra's eyes narrowed. "Oh? Just today? Seems like you've gone through a box of tissues an hour for the past week."

"I know," Ali admitted. "My hormones must be out of whack. I've been tearing up over really stupid things lately. Like last night. Luke gave me a kiss and told me he loved me—he does that every night before we go to bed—and I just started blubbering. Bizarre."

"Not so bizarre if you're pregnant," Audra said.

Ali's gaze flew to Ree, who held up her hands. "Hey, don't look at me. Audra's the expert on pregnancy."

"I'm not pregnant," Ali said. But then her eyes widened. "I can't be…"

She sat in silence for a moment, holding out her hands as her lips and fingers moved simultaneously.

"Doing the math, huh?" Audra chuckled.

"Oh, my."

"You could buy one of those little kits at the drug-store," Ree suggested.

"Yes," Audra seconded. "I'll pick one up after we leave here." She chuckled again. "Won't the clerk at the pharmacy get a kick out of seeing me belly-up to the cash register with one of those things?"

Ali worried her lower lip. "What if Luke decides to come home early?"

"We'll go to my house. I'll make sure Seth keeps Mom and Dad out of our hair for a while. You'll know for sure in short order and then tonight you can make Luke the happiest man on the planet. Well, the happiest man besides Seth, of course."

"Sounds like a plan," Ali said, smiling.

Ree was smiling, too, until Audra said, "Speaking of happy men, Dane seemed to have a little more spring in his step today."

Ree gave the lunch menu her full attention. "How is your chef's pasta primavera?" she asked, eager to change the subject.

"Excellent, but we're talking about Dane."

Ree's gaze shifted to Ali, hoping to garner support, but the other woman shrugged. "Aud's a nosy pain in the butt most of the time, but in this case I'm a little curious myself to find out what's going on between you and our brother."

"Nothing is going on," she said, but even to her own ears, her tone lacked conviction.

"The windows in the conference room nearly fogged up, Ree," Ali said dryly. "People pay dating services good money to encounter that kind of nothing."

Ree felt her cheeks heating with mortification. After all, Ali and Audra knew she was married. She could only imagine what they thought of her interest in their brother.

"I really care about him," she said, even though it went well beyond that. "But we're…that is, we've…"

At a loss for how to explain her feelings and their relationship, she picked up her water glass and sipped.

Audra's expression held understanding. "Look, Ree, even though you've never said anything about the situation with your husband, we kind of know."

"You do."

"Dane told me that you're separated."

"And Aud mentioned it to me," Ali inserted.

"But even if Dane hadn't said a word, it was pretty obvious your marriage was in trouble. Your husband isn't around and you never talk about him the way most married women talk about their husbands." She pointed to Ree's unadorned hand. "You don't wear a ring."

"Yeah," Ali said. "And then there's the way the

resort's sprinkler system goes off whenever you and Dane are in the conference room together."

"I've moved ahead with the divorce. I should have ended things permanently two years ago," she admitted quietly.

Audra's head bobbed once in a nod. "You weren't ready two years ago. You are now."

"So, what are your intentions toward our big brother?" Ali asked on a wink.

Ree wasn't expecting company, so when the bell rang on Sunday afternoon, she walked to the front door on her heels with cotton balls tucked between her toes to keep from smudging the fresh coat of polish she'd just applied to her nails.

Dane grinned as he glanced down at her feet. "Nice," he murmured. "Reminds me of cotton candy. I've always loved the stuff. Very…tasty."

"I can do yours next, if you'd like."

His eyebrows rose. "I'd rather apply a second coat for you."

"This is still wet. It will take another couple minutes to dry."

"Or less if I blow on them."

She shivered in the open doorway. The temperature outside was hovering in the forties. But that wasn't what had raised gooseflesh on her arms.

"Are you going to invite me in?" Dane asked.

"Of course." She stepped back. "I'm surprised to see you today." But glad, even though if she had known he was coming she would have dressed in something more flattering than faded jeans and an old flannel work shirt that had belonged to her grandfather.

"I probably could have called, but I figured it would be more fun to deliver this news in person."

"What news?"

"I'm an uncle." He pulled a pink bubblegum cigar from the back pocket of his jeans and handed it to Ree. "Aud gave birth at 7:46 last night."

"Congratulations!" Ree squealed. "Come on, spill. I want all the details."

He rubbed his chin. "Let's see, the baby weighed in at seven pounds and some odd change and measures nearly twenty inches. She's bald as a peeled egg, but then I don't think Audra had any hair to speak of till she was about two."

"Who does she look like?"

"Hard to say. She kind of resembles Winston Churchill."

"God, you're terrible." Ree swatted his arm. "What did they name her?"

"LeeAnn, after Seth's sister." He turned serious then. "She's something else."

"I can't wait to see her," Ree said.

"Actually that's why I stopped by. Audra wanted me to tell you that she'd love for you to come up if you're free today. I'm on my way back to the hospital now. I thought I'd swing by, see if you wanted to go."

Deeply touched to be included, Ree grinned. "Just let me change."

* * *

"Ree! You made it," Audra called out when they entered the hospital room.

Seth sat next to her on the bed. Both of them were beaming despite looking utterly exhausted.

Even though the hospital's policy only allowed a couple visitors at a time, the room was packed. Ali sat in the rocking chair, a pink-wrapped bundle in her arms. Luke was behind the rocker, making cooing noises over his wife's shoulder. An older couple stood near the window. Dane's parents, she decided, even before he began the introductions.

"Mom and Dad, this is Regina Bellini."

"We've heard a lot about you," Mrs. Conlan said. She had been rearranging the vases of flowers that were lined up on the windowsill. She stopped now to step forward and shake Ree's hand.

Even though Beth Conlan's smile was friendly and her words hardly an indictment, Ree still felt on trial.

Mr. Conlan shook her hand as well. When he smiled, that same solitary dimple that dented Dane's cheek, tugged in on his. Half a dozen real cigars peeked out of the breast pocket of his plaid shirt. He held one out to Ree.

"Nice to meet you. Have a stogie."

"Thanks. And same here. Congratulations." Ree glanced around the room motioning with the cigar. "To all of you."

Every one of the Conlans was present and accounted for, welcoming the newest addition to their brood with wide smiles and eyes full of pride. Ree was awed by their closeness, and she envied it as well. They didn't know how lucky they were. Then again, she thought, maybe they did and that's why they were all here, celebrating this special occasion together.

Unable to resist any longer, Ree walked over for her first peek at the baby in Ali's arms. Beneath a little pink stocking cap, a pair of sleepy eyes tried to focus before giving up and closing. Ree felt her heart swell and the old desires for family grew right along with it. Someday, she thought. Someday. This time, the inexact date was not nearly so troubling.

"Are you going to hog that baby all afternoon, Alice?" Beth Conlan demanded.

"I'm thinking about it."

"You know, if you'd get busy and give me a second grandbaby, we would each have one to hold," Dane's mother stated boldly.

The lunch conversation from the other day played back through Ree's head. She hadn't gone to Audra's when Ali took the pregnancy test, but she knew the results now by the way Ali glanced lovingly over her shoulder at Luke, whose face lit up with a grin more dazzling than the Rockefeller Center Christmas tree.

"You can stop harping, Mom. Luke and I are already on that. About the time LeeAnn starts crawling, we'll be setting her up with a cousin."

Pandemonium broke out then. Hugs were exchanged, backs slapped, happy sentiments offered. Ree stepped back content to be on the periphery of the excitement, and not wanting to intrude, but Ali reeled her back in with an offer to hold LeeAnn.

"Come on, Ree. Take her. It's your turn."

"Oh, no. Let Mrs. Conlan have her first," she demurred, even as her fingers itched to touch the baby's soft skin and feel that comforting weight in her arms.

But Ali was shaking her head. "Once Mom gets hold of her no one else is going to get a chance for the rest of the day. Come on."

Ree glanced around uneasily. All eyes seemed to be on her. "Well, okay."

She traded spots with Ali and sighed contentedly when the baby was tucked into her arms.

"Oh, look at you," she cooed, forgetting all about being self-conscious when one tiny fist poked up from the receiving blanket. Ree held out her index finger, chuckling softly when LeeAnn grasped it.

"Isn't she something?" Dane murmured proudly as he squatted down beside the chair.

"Amazing."

She turned her head to grin at Dane, who smiled back. Their gazes locked, lingered. A silent message that brimmed with hope seemed to pass between them. When Ree glanced over his shoulder, she caught Dane's parents trading a look as well. This one brimmed with both speculation…and concern.

Now that his mother had met Regina, Dane expected to get the third degree. The only surprise was that she waited nearly two weeks before doing so. During that time, she'd managed to bump into Ree twice, just *happening* to be at the resort when their usual Friday meeting about the Victorian's renovations took place.

Both times, Dane had held his breath. It was important, so important, that his parents see her as he did: a smart and good-hearted woman who was determined to carve out a new and happy life for herself.

The family was gathered around Audra's kitchen table for Sunday dinner. His mother had prepared roast beef, mashed potatoes and green bean casserole. The menu was a little more pedestrian now that Audra had delivered LeeAnn. Even so, Dane gladly helped himself to seconds, all while eyeing the apple cobbler that was still cooling on the counter. After dinner, he planned to settle on the couch in the den with a slice of it to watch the rest of the Lion's game with the guys on Seth's big screen television.

He never made it out of the kitchen.

"Your father and I would like to have a word with you, Dane Michael," his mom said.

Even though he was halfway through his thirties, the use of his middle name had warning bells sounding in his head. His father's pained sigh didn't alleviate his trepidation.

"Beth, let it be. I thought we agreed we wouldn't say anything?"

"We agreed? I never agreed. We're his parents. It's our job to say something," she finished smartly.

"He's a grown man."

Sure, Dane thought, a grown man who was being talked about as if he wasn't even in the room. He noted the grim line of his mother's mouth, though, and decided not to give voice to that observation.

"You don't need to stay," she told his father, even though the look on her face clearly said she expected him to.

His father was either being very brave or very foolish, Dane decided, when he eagerly cleared out with his sons-in-law. Audra and Ali, of course, had to be shooed from the room. Even then, Dane was pretty sure they were hovering somewhere nearby, eavesdropping.

He settled back into his chair at the table. "Is something wrong, Mom?" he asked innocently.

"I wasn't going to bring this up," she began, and Dane heard a muffled snort of laughter from just outside the door. Every lecture he could remember from his teen years on had begun this way. She shot a black look in the direction of the door before continuing. "But I've heard some things and…well, I've got eyes."

"What is it, Mom?"

"Are you carrying on with a married woman?"

"No!" Despite the denial, he felt heat flame into his cheeks.

He knew his mother saw it, too, when she said, "Dane Michael Conlan, your father and I raised you better than this."

"Mom, Ree and I are not…carrying on," he replied emphatically.

"They're not, Mom," Ali called from the hallway. "If they were, he wouldn't be so frustrated and moody."

"If I want to listen to that kind of coarse talk, Alice Marie, I'll turn on cable, thank you very much," their mother admonished. "You and Audra go check on the baby and give us some privacy."

Dane couldn't help snickering when he heard two muffled, "Yes, ma'ams."

Still, any hope he'd harbored that the topic was now

closed withered quickly as his mother launched into a five-minute lecture on the sanctity of marriage.

Afterward Dane said quietly, "Mom, I know how the situation must look to you, but Ree's separated from her husband and getting a divorce. They haven't lived together in more than two years."

"That doesn't make her single."

"No, but I haven't done anything wrong and neither has she." He reached for the pie to break off a piece of flaky crust, only to have his hand slapped.

"What happened to Julie? She was such a nice girl."

"She is nice. She's just not…" Ree, he thought.

"I don't want to see you hurt," Beth Conlan said. She laid a hand against his cheek, the same hand that had checked for fevers and bandaged scraped knees.

"How can I be hurt?" He took his mom's hand and gave it a reassuring squeeze. "Regina and I aren't even officially dating."

"But you love her."

Dane swallowed, waiting for the denial that never made it past his lips. Love? He hadn't said that word aloud. He hadn't allowed himself to think it in context with Ree. But that's what he felt all right.

He'd always considered himself a patient man, levelheaded and in control. He'd been anything but since that first, fateful meeting. He wanted Ree. More than just wanting her, he wanted to be with her.

Forever.

"She's the one, Mom," he said, accepting the truth at last. "She's the one I've been waiting for."

"And if you have to keep waiting?"

The prospect had his gut clenching, but his tone was firm when he said, "I will. She's worth it."

CHAPTER TEN

IT WAS Thanksgiving Day, but Dane was humming "Winter Wonderland" as he jogged up the Victorian's front steps, his breath wreathing white around him in the frigid November air. It had snowed overnight, a light dusting that turned the bare tree branches into something magical.

Or maybe that was just how he felt because he would be spending the day with Regina, celebrating what he hoped would be the first of many holidays together. The past couple weeks had been perfect...as perfect as they could be under the current circumstances. They'd spent every day and part of every evening together laughing, talking, sharing meals.

Soon, Dane told himself, their self-imposed look-but-don't-touch restrictions would be lifted. Soon, they would be free to talk about more than what the future held for the house they were restoring.

He knocked once on the door's oval of stained glass and tucked his hands into the pockets of his leather jacket. He should have worn a heavier coat, he thought, while he waited for her to answer. The plan was to first hit the parade that snaked down Trillium's main street and then head to Audra's house, where his family was assembling for the day's feast.

Ree had insisted she would bring a dish as well. He'd gone to the grocery store with her the evening before, nearly expiring from desire as she'd picked out the ingredients for one of her nonna's recipes. He got the feeling she knew damned well how much her Italian inflection turned him on when she'd leaned over and seductively whispered "oregano" in his ear.

Despite her continued concern, Beth Conlan had been the one to issue the invitation. No one should be alone on a holiday intended to celebrate sharing and friendship, his mother had said.

When the door opened, Regina smiled, but her expression was tight and she seemed oddly apprehensive.

"Happy Thanksgiving," Dane said. Giving in to impulse, he leaned forward to kiss her cheek. He wanted to indulge in much more than that solitary, innocent peck. Not yet, though. Not yet.

She glanced over her shoulder nervously—guiltily?—before wishing him the same in return. Then, despite not having on a coat, she stepped outside. "I tried to catch you before you left your house and you didn't answer your cell. I…I need to talk to you."

"Can we talk in the truck?" He hitched a thumb over his shoulder, impatient to be off. "The parade starts in less than an hour and we're going to miss the next ferry if we dawdle too long."

"This can't wait." She wrapped her arms around herself, shivered.

"Well, at least let's go inside. It's freezing out here."

"No, Dane. I—"

But he reached around her to open the door. "This is ridiculous, Ree. You're shaking." With a gentle nudge, he backed her inside.

And then Dane felt as if he had stepped into a bad dream. A pair of men's shoes was on the rug, right next to a large suitcase. Atop the suitcase rested a hat, wide-rimmed and dust-covered, the kind that would keep the sun out of a man's eyes while he worked to unearth fossils and other artifacts in the desert. Dane had seen enough, and yet his gaze moved on to the coat tree in the corner of the foyer and the weathered men's jacket that hung from its limbs. Dane's heart bucked once against his ribs and then seemed to skitter to a halt. All the markings of the husband he had once looked for in Regina's home were there now.

"Ree?" He glanced over in question and saw her swallow hard.

"Paul arrived this morning."

"Your husband is here?"

"Don't call him that," she pleaded quietly.

How else should Dane refer to the other man? His thoughts turned grim then. Other man? Chaste as their relationship had been, Dane supposed, technically, that would be him.

"What does he want?" He asked the question, but he figured he knew. Paul Ritter had returned for his wife.

"He—"

The man in question walked into view then. His hair, blond and a little long, was damp from a shower and he was still fastening the buttons on his shirt. He blinked in surprise when he spotted Dane.

"Hello. I didn't realize we had company," he said. He held out a hand, eyes crinkling into an absent smile behind wire-rimmed glasses. "I'm Paul Ritter."

"Dane Conlan."

"Nice to meet you." He turned to Ree then. "Where do you keep the aspirin? I've got a killer headache." For Dane's benefit, he added, "I've been traveling all night. The airport was a zoo with people all wanting to get home today."

Thanksgiving Day.

The scene was so damningly domestic, Dane knew he had to leave and leave quickly. Even though he wanted to demand an explanation, the bitter fact remained: He wasn't entitled to one. And that hurt. God, that hurt.

"I...I just stopped by to wish Ree a happy Thanksgiving." It took a Herculean effort to push the words past his stiff lips. "We...we're work associates."

Ree glanced at him sharply. She looked as if he'd slapped her. Dane regretted that, but he was too gut-punched, too heart-gouged to sooth her wounded feelings.

He intended to leave quickly, to put as much distance between himself and this painful scene as possible, but Ree followed him outside and jogged down the steps after him.

"Dane! Dane!" she hollered. She reached for his hand. Her fingers felt as cold as his heart when they weaved through his. "Please don't go. Not like this."

"How else should I leave? Should I walk away smiling, Ree? Your husband is back. And I've...I've got no right to be here."

No right to be here, no right to love her. And yet he did. His heart wasn't just breaking. It was shattering into unsalvageable pieces. And to think he'd once envied his sisters this kind of fathomless emotion. Well, he wanted no part of it now. He pulled his hand free.

"My soon-to-be *ex*-husband," she stressed. "He got in this morning from Nevada after a long flight, and then just showed up here." She shook her head in what appeared to be exasperation. "He didn't even realize it was Thanksgiving Day. Paul's always been scattered like that."

Dane felt marginally better knowing the man had not hightailed it home to be with his wife for the holiday, but that didn't change the fact that he was back and obviously planned to stay.

"Not so scattered that he forgot to pack. His luggage is in your foyer. It looks like he intends to be here awhile."

"I agreed to let him shower. That's the extent of it. He'll be leaving shortly. He knows I've made plans for the day."

Dane glanced back at the house. "Under the circumstances, I don't think those plans are valid any longer."

"I want to spend the day with you," she said quietly.

Dane rubbed his eyes with the heels of his hands. He couldn't keep the frustration out of his tone when he snapped, "I want much more than a day, Ree. Haven't you figured that out by now?"

Her smile was at odds with the tears glimmering in her eyes. "I'd hoped. I…I want that, too."

Where exactly did that leave them?

The question must have been visible in his expression, because she murmured, "It will just be a little longer. I promise."

"A little longer," he repeated and paced the rest of the distance to his vehicle. Before lifting the door handle, he asked, "Has he signed the divorce papers?"

"No." She sighed heavily and walked to his side. "He...he came to Michigan to discuss them. He wants—"

"His wife."

"No, dammit, it's not like that." She shook her head violently. "Why won't you listen?"

"Because maybe it should be like that," Dane replied with a defeated sigh. He turned and pointed to the window where another man now stood watching this scene. Where another man stood waiting for Regina. "Maybe Paul has finally figured out what I know—you're incredible, Ree. You're sexy, smart, beautiful. You're passionate in the best sense of the word. He'd be lost without you in his life. Absolutely and irrevocably lost."

He touched her cheek, following the streak of her tears with his index finger. "I know," he said softly. "I know that's how he would feel, because that's how I feel."

"Oh, Dane."

She stepped toward him, but he shook his head, and opened the door to his Trailblazer.

"I need to go now, Ree."

She had no choice but to let him. Long after Dane left, she stood in the driveway. The frigid wind slapped at her, but that wasn't why she felt so bruised and chilled. I need to go, Dane had told her. He'd never said when or even if he would be back.

The door opened behind her. "Ree?" Paul called.

She wanted to ask him to give her a minute, but then,

straightening her spine, she decided against it. She had postponed too many things over the years, thinking that by not confronting them she could avoid heartache or disappointment or feeling like a failure. It was time to face the past if she hoped to have any chance at the future that she had so recently begun to believe might be possible.

"Let's go in the kitchen," she said. "I'll make a fresh pot of coffee and we can talk."

Paul nodded.

"So, that the guy who bought the house?" he asked once they were seated at the table.

"Yes."

"From the look on his face, I'd say he considers you to be more than—what was the phrase he used?—um, a work associate."

He wasn't trying to be cruel. Paul didn't care deeply enough to do that. But Ree's heart absorbed the hit anyway.

"Let's leave Dane out of this, okay?" She took a deep breath, let it out slowly. "I want to talk about the divorce papers and what it will take to get you to finally sign them."

Paul steepled his fingers under his chin and nodded in that distracted way of his, looking more like a professor about to launch into a lecture on some obscure finding than a husband facing the dissolution of his marriage.

"I'll sign them, but I think we need to discuss the terms of our settlement first."

"Fine. That's easy enough. As I told you when I first left I don't want anything from you. I think it's fair that we leave the marriage with what we brought to it. As for what we accumulated jointly, there's nothing of significant value."

Paul's bland expression sharpened. "Actually there is. In the letter I received from Bradley Townsend, he was willing to pay a handsome sum for this house and property. The letter took some time to reach me at the dig site and by the time it had, you'd already sold the house. I'm assuming Dane Conlan offered a similar amount."

She blinked in surprise, irritation doing battle with her sudden uneasiness over the turn their conversation had taken.

"The house was mine outright, Paul. My grandmother left it to me. What I sold it for is none of your business. The inheritance laws of this state are clear on that."

"When it comes to money, the law is never clear," he replied.

She couldn't believe it. Paul had never cared about money. They'd lived on a shoestring budget for all of their marriage, every extra penny poured back into his chronically underfunded work.

"What are you saying?"

"I'll sign the papers." He pushed the glasses up the bridge of his nose. "I'll do it today if you'll agree to give me half the Victorian's purchase price."

"I'll do no such thing." He wasn't entitled to half of all her grandparents had worked so doggedly to achieve. This visit marked only the second time he'd set foot in the Victorian.

"Then you'll leave me no choice but to contest the divorce. Things could drag on for months, maybe longer while the courts decide the matter."

She didn't know if he was bluffing or not. All she knew was that her future with Dane was becoming more complicated by the minute. Would he be willing to wait that long? Or would he decide she wasn't worth the grief?

"Why, Paul?" she asked, bewildered. "You've never struck me as materialistic. You would have signed the papers before if you'd remembered to get around to it."

He actually had the audacity to reach across the table and pat her hand.

"Here's the thing, Ree, the economy being what it is, the foundation sponsoring our dig has decided to scale back its funding for next year. We're going to have to pull out early if we don't get some extra cash. Even then, I'm going to have to let half the team go."

"This is about work? It's about a stinking dig?" Ree asked incredulously. She almost laughed then, but the situation was too pathetic to warrant humor. Dane—noble, honorable man that he was—had stepped back for *this?*

"What did you think?" Paul asked, and the blank and baffled look on his face, fired up Ree's temper.

"I think you'd better get out of Dane's house."

Audra and Ali stopped by the following afternoon, bringing Ree leftover turkey and the trimmings, including Beth Conlan's homemade pumpkin pie.

"We missed you at dinner yesterday," Audra said as she nursed LeeAnn. They were seated around the kitchen table.

"I wanted to be there. Something unexpected came up," Ree hedged. Then she decided to just spill it. "The truth is, my husband showed up. Dane...Dane was pretty upset when he left here."

"He was pretty upset when he got to my house, too," Audra replied. "He told us you wouldn't be coming, although he didn't give us a reason, and then he left. He didn't even stay for dinner."

Ree closed her eyes, but the tears leaked out anyway. They had both spent the holiday alone and miserable. It wasn't fair.

"I'm sorry, Ree." Ali reached over to give her arm a squeeze. "It's going to be okay. I know things must seem bad right now, but you and Dane will work this out."

"I don't know." And Ree meant it. "I've tried phoning him—last night and this morning. I keep getting his answering machine and he hasn't returned my calls."

"He just needs time," Audra said.

"Time," Ree sighed. She was beginning to hate that word.

"What did your husband want?" Ali asked.

That was the kicker, she thought. "Well, Dane figured Paul was back for me and so he decided he was just going to bow out gracefully." She sighed heavily. "I love your brother, but God, sometimes his sense of honor can be damned annoying.

"But the truth is that Paul wants half the money Saybrook's gave me for the house." Her laugh was bitter. "He said he needs it to go chasing more fossils. And if I don't give it to him, he'll contest the divorce."

"It's a little late for that, isn't it?" Audra said at the same time Ali asked, "Can he do that?"

Ree sighed heavily. "I don't know. I haven't been

able to reach my lawyer because of the holiday week-end, but I think he may be able to do it. I think he still had time to respond to the last batch of paperwork. Part of me is tempted just to give him the money and send him on his way."

"Is that what you told him?"

She smiled now. "No. I told him to go to hell—right after I told him to get out of Dane's house. He hasn't wanted anything to do with me or our marriage for years. He shouldn't profit from my grandparents' hard work now."

Ree took those words to heart as winter began in earnest and the weeks passed. Dane had retreated not just emotionally, but physically. It was now Ali who came on Tuesdays, Wednesdays and Thursdays to work with Regina and Case Portman on the Victorian's restoration.

As the new year got under way, so did the home's new look. The upstairs bedrooms were rewired to bring them up to code and their walls were in the process of being patched and replastered, after which fresh paint would be applied. Ree had chosen the colors, pairing muted roses with rich burgundies, and pale blues, greens and golds. The paint would coordinate with wallpaper borders, window treatments, throw rugs and bedding.

Ree felt a sense of satisfaction as she watched the old floors being sanded and refinished until the wood gleamed. But her heart still ached. She'd only heard from Dane twice since Thanksgiving.

The first was a note that Ali delivered that first Tuesday on which she'd showed up at the house in his stead.

"I think it's for the best, until current circumstances

change, that we don't see one another," the brief missive read. Only the fact that he'd signed it "Love, Dane" kept her from panicking.

The second communication arrived the day before Christmas along with the delivery of a fully furnished dollhouse—an exact replica of the one they'd seen in the shop that day in Petoskey. It's exterior had been painted the same colors Ree had chosen for the outside of her Victorian. The card read: "So you'll always have your home."

As the months slipped by and her divorce inched forward at a maddeningly slow pace, Ree comforted herself with the thought that the home she really wanted was one with Dane.

"Work on the house is really clipping along," Ali said as she sat in Dane's office on the second Thursday in May.

He flipped absently through the stack of photos she'd provided, only half paying attention. He hadn't been able to concentrate on much of anything in months. He missed Ree, even though he knew that avoiding her was for the best. She apparently agreed. She no longer came to Saybrook's on Fridays to offer an update on the restoration. Ali was doing that for her now.

"Cole says the new windows he ordered for the tower room should be installed by next week at the latest," his sister was saying.

"Great."

And, because he didn't want to appear completely out of it, Dane decided he'd better ask some questions. So, for the next couple minutes Ali patiently answered his inquiries about chimney repairs and the new kitchen appliances that had been ordered. But then she put her hands on her hips and sighed in exasperation.

"Why don't you ask me about Ree instead of pretending you give a damn about the condition of the flue in the parlor fireplace?"

Staying away from her was killing him, but it had to be this way. When she was free—if that ever happened—he would go to her. Until then, he needed to keep his distance in order to hold on to what remained of his sanity and self-respect.

He rubbed his eyes now. And because he did want to know, he asked, "Is she okay?"

His sister had told him that Paul was long gone from the house and that, although he was contesting the divorce, Ree was moving ahead with it. Dane wanted to give the other guy a well-deserved poke in the eye for basically trying to extort money from her. And, while part of him wanted to just pay Paul whatever amount it would take to make him go away, Dane respected Ree for holding firm. The man didn't deserve money—whether he planned to use it to finance a dig or blow it on gambling. It was the principle of the matter.

"She's doing about as well as you are," Ali replied. "Why don't you go see her?"

"You know why." He rubbed his eyes. A night of quality sleep was a long forgotten luxury. "I don't want to just *see* her, Al. I don't want to be her boss or her friend or anything else that platonic and impermanent. I want to be her husband. And until that position is vacant, I…I can't spend time with her and pretend otherwise."

"I know," Ali said, coming around the desk to give him a hug.

She was just straightening when Audra walked into his office holding a package the size of a shirt box that was decked out in festive paper and a bow.

"It came special delivery," she said, excitement brimming in her blue eyes as she handed it to him. "The return address is Ree's."

That announcement had his mouth going dry.

"It's awfully light," he remarked, his curiosity mounting as he tugged off the bow and peeled back the paper.

When he lifted the top and saw the contents, his heart lurched into his throat and he lurched out of his seat. Even so, he somehow managed to choke out the words, "If anyone needs me, I'll be out of the office for the rest of the afternoon."

He was out the door before they could even open their mouths.

"My God! What got into him?" Audra said.

Ali was more practical than to ask questions. She reached into the box and snatched out the documents nestled inside.

"I'll be damned," she murmured, breaking into a grin as she read the top sheet.

"What is this?" Audra asked.

"Regina's divorce decree."

Ree was expecting Dane or at least hoping outrageously that he would arrive once he received the delivery she'd arranged for that afternoon.

So she was standing in the bay window, watching the

fat thunderclouds gather, when his truck pulled up the driveway. She'd lit candles, half a dozen of them. They burned on every available surface in the Victorian's newly refurbished and furnished front parlor. Music, soft and slow, played on the stereo. She'd already uncorked the champagne—again being hopeful.

But then her heart did a little dive when she opened the door to his neutral expression. She'd expected a smile, maybe even laughter. Instead all she got was a dry, "Hello."

"Did you get my…message?" she asked cautiously.

"I got it." Something flickered in his eyes and she thought, for just a moment, she saw that dimple wink before he asked, "New dress?"

"Uh-huh." She smoothed the fabric over her hips. "Do you like it?"

It took an effort not to fidget as his frank gaze swept down the length of her, lingering for a moment where the neckline scooped low.

"It looks good on you," he said on a nod.

"Thanks. I bought it this afternoon. I…I felt like celebrating."

She still couldn't quite gauge his mood.

"You put your hair up."

"Yes." As her heart hammered, she added, "I thought you might like to take it down."

His eyebrows arched and this time she knew she saw the dimple, but Dane remained on the porch, a good arm's length away.

"So, how does it feel to be a single woman?" he asked in a maddeningly conversational tone.

"Good…great."

"Well, don't get used to it." And, finally, he reached for her.

Regina melted into his arms on a laugh that turned into a sob. He was laughing, too, his eyes just as bright, his heart beating just as unsteadily against hers. This was where she wanted to stay forever, encircled in his arms, near to his heart.

"God, I've missed you, Ree. These past months have been hell. You—being with you—it's all I've thought about, dreamed about."

"I know, I know. Me, too,"

"I love you, Ree."

"I love you, too."

Lightning scored the cloudy May sky as he lowered his head to kiss her with all the passion that had been forbidden before. Thunder rent the afternoon's silence and the rain that had been threatening to fall all day finally came down in a gushing torrent as the kiss ended.

Ree grinned, feeling insanely happy in spite of nature's furious assault.

"This is where it all began," she mused. "Right here. Just like this."

"No." Dane scooped her up in his arms, carrying her over the threshold and then kicking the freshly painted door closed with the heel of his shoe. It would leave a mark, but that was okay. Memories sometimes did.

The kiss he gave her now was infused with impatience, but the words that followed it were spoken slowly and with thrilling conviction.

"*This* is where it begins."

EPILOGUE

GUESTS milled about inside the gorgeously restored Victorian. They sauntered over the lawn and through the newly planted flower gardens, admiring the blooms. They traversed the wooden boardwalk down near Lake Michigan and swayed to the music on the dance floor that had been erected near the gazebo.

Saybrook's on the Pointe would not open officially until the fall, but on this sunny summer afternoon, it was hosting a wedding reception.

Dane sat with his bride in the gazebo, taking a break from the dancing. Audra and Seth sat across from them, beaming proudly as LeeAnn pulled herself up to standing and managed a few steps while holding on to the seat.

"Did you see her? Did you see her?" Audra shouted excitedly and gave Seth a quick kiss. "Eight months old and already walking. Can you beat that?"

The question was rhetorical, but Ali answered it anyway. "Maybe." Patting the mound of her stomach, she added, "I think I've been having contractions for the past couple of hours."

While the others grinned, Luke paled beneath his tan. "Con-contractions?"

"Uh-huh. They're getting a little stronger and a little closer together. I think this might be it." She sounded a little nervous and a lot excited.

Luke helped her to her feet and the others gathered around her, offering hugs and encouragement.

"Let's have one last toast," Dane said. He poured more champagne in their glasses, skipping Ali's since she still had some club soda left from earlier.

The Conlans stood in a circle in the gazebo, a circle made larger and more complete thanks to love.

"Here's to forgiveness," Audra said and Seth nodded.

"Homecomings," Luke murmured.

"Reunions," Ali added.

"How about honor and patience," Ree said, smiling at her new husband, but she thought Dane summed it up best with his toast.

"Here's to family."

* * * * *

The next book in
THE BRIDES OF BELLA LUCIA *series*
is out next month!
Don't miss THE REBEL PRINCE by Raye Morgan

Here's an exclusive sneak preview of
Emma Valentine's story!

"OH, NO!"

The reaction slipped out before Emma Valentine could stop it, for there stood the very man she most wanted to avoid seeing again.

He didn't look any happier to see her.

"Well, come on, get on board," he said gruffly. "I won't bite." One eyebrow rose. "Though I might nibble a little," he added, mostly to amuse himself.

But she wasn't paying any attention to what he was saying. She was staring at him, taking in the royal blue uniform he was wearing, with gold braid and glistening badges decorating the sleeves, epaulettes and an upright collar. Ribbons and medals covered the breast of the short, fitted jacket. A gold-encrusted sabre hung at his side. And suddenly it was clear to her who this man really was.

She gulped wordlessly. Reaching out, he took her elbow and pulled her aboard. The doors slid closed. And finally she found her tongue.

"You…you're the prince."

He nodded, barely glancing at her. "Yes. Of course."

She raised a hand and covered her mouth for a moment. "I should have known."

"Of course you should have. I don't know why you didn't." He punched the ground-floor button to get the elevator moving again, then turned to look down at her. "A relatively bright five-year-old child would have tumbled to the truth right away."

Her shock faded as her indignation at his tone asserted itself. He might be the prince, but he was still just as annoying as he had been earlier that day.

"A relatively bright five-year-old child without a bump on the head from a badly thrown water polo ball, maybe," she said defensively. She wasn't feeling woozy any longer and she wasn't about to let him bully her, no matter how royal he was. "I was unconscious half the time."

"And just clueless the other half, I guess," he said, looking bemused.

The arrogance of the man was really galling.

"I suppose you think your 'royalness' is so obvious it sort of shimmers around you for all to see?" she challenged. "Or better yet, oozes from your pores like…like sweat on a hot day?"

"Something like that," he acknowledged calmly. "Most people tumble to it pretty quickly. In fact, it's hard to hide even when I want to avoid dealing with it."

"Poor baby," she said, still resenting his manner. "I guess that works better with injured people who are half asleep." Looking at him, she felt a strange emotion she couldn't identify. It was as though she wanted to prove something to him, but she wasn't sure what. "And anyway, you know you did your best to fool me," she added.

His brows knit together as though he really didn't know what she was talking about. "I didn't do a thing."

"You told me your name was Monty."

"It is." He shrugged. "I have a lot of names. Some of them are too rude to be spoken to my face, I'm sure." He glanced at her sideways, his hand on the hilt of his sabre. "Perhaps you're contemplating one of those right now."

You bet I am.

That was what she would like to say. But it suddenly occurred to her that she was supposed to be working for this man. If she wanted to keep the job of coronation chef, maybe she'd better keep her opinions to herself. So she clamped her mouth shut, took a deep breath and looked away, trying hard to calm down.

The elevator ground to a halt and the doors slid open laboriously. She moved to step forward, hoping to make her escape, but his hand shot out again and caught her elbow.

"Wait a minute. *You're* a woman," he said, as though that thought had just presented itself to him.

"That's a rare ability for insight you have there, Your Highness," she snapped before she could stop herself. And then she winced. She was going to have to do better than that if she was going to keep this relationship on an even keel.

But he was ignoring her dig. Nodding, he stared at her with a speculative gleam in his golden eyes. "I've been looking for a woman, but you'll do."

She blanched, stiffening. "I'll do for what?"

He made a head gesture in a direction she knew was opposite of where she was going and his grip tightened on her elbow.

"Come with me," he said abruptly, making it an order.

She dug in her heels, thinking fast. She didn't much like orders. "Wait! I can't. I have to get to the kitchen."

"Not yet. I need you."

"You what?" Her breathless gasp of surprise was soft, but she knew he'd heard it.

"I need you," he said firmly. "Oh, don't look so shocked. I'm not planning to throw you into the hay and have my way with you. I need you for something a bit more mundane than that."

She felt color rushing into her cheeks and she silently begged it to stop. Here she was, formless and stodgy in her chef's whites. No makeup, no stiletto heels. Hardly the picture of the femmes fatales he was undoubtedly used to. The likelihood that he would have any carnal interest in her was remote at best. To have him think she was hysterically defending her virtue was humiliating.

"Well, what if I don't want to go with you?" she said in hopes of deflecting his attention from her blush.

"Too bad."

"What?"

Amusement sparkled in his eyes. He was certainly enjoying this. And that only made her more determined to resist him.

"I'm the prince, remember? And we're in the castle. My orders take precedence. It's that old pesky divine rights thing."

Her jaw jutted out. Despite her embarrassment, she couldn't let that pass.

"Over my free will? Never!"

Exasperation filled his face.

"Hey, call out the historians. Someone will write a book about you and your courageous principles." His eyes glittered sardonically. "But in the meantime, Emma Valentine, you're coming with me."

Page-turning drama...

Exotic, glamorous locations...

Intense emotion and passionate seduction...

Sheikhs, princes and billionaire tycoons...

This summer, may we suggest:

THE SHEIKH'S DISOBEDIENT BRIDE
by Jane Porter
On sale June.

AT THE GREEK TYCOON'S BIDDING
by Cathy Williams
On sale July.

THE ITALIAN MILLIONAIRE'S VIRGIN WIFE
On sale August.

With new titles to choose from every month,
discover a world of romance in our books written
by internationally bestselling authors.

HARLEQUIN® *Presents*

It's the ultimate in quality romance!

Available wherever Harlequin books are sold.

www.eHarlequin.com

HPGEN06